CEORFAN TEENS

A CEORFAN GARGOYLE NOVELLA

MIKI WARD
GARRETT WARD

Cover design provided by Christina Schneider at Miki and Mine LLC/Editing by
Erica Collins
Formatted by Vicki M Duran

NOTE FROM THE AUTHORS

We dedicate this book to all the romantic firecrackers out there.
-Miki & Garrett

TO OUR READERS ...

Thank you for purchasing this book and reading it! Please don't be afraid to leave a review if you like it. This book is shorter than the novels in the Ceorfan Gargoyles Series and is a stand-alone novella. It is concentrated on a few of the characters from the series and their unique points of view. It might contain mild violence and language.

Sincerely yours,
Miki & Garrett Ward

1

MEETING THE QB

It's a warm day even if it's February, and I'm sweating through my blue cheerleading practice shorts and white tee. The other girls look beautiful, they always do.

Maureen, or Tween as we call our captain, puts a hand up and calls us over to the bleachers. Her caramel blond ponytail bouncing with her movement. She's a pretty girl but intelligent too. When we get situated in our seats, she gives us instructions for the game this weekend.

"The game Friday after next is only a scrimmage. I know you already know the season is over but treat this like a regular game. It's important the players know we're behind them so next season they start like champions. Wear your blue uniforms with the tan leggings. I want you sexed up and ready. Now, who's ready?" Tween shouts getting us pumped up with her own excitement.

We jump up, shouting, "We are!" We put our hands in a pile and hum loudly raising them then roar, "Goooo, Cave Bears."

With practice over, we break apart, and everyone goes our separate ways. A dark-haired beauty with almost black eyes, Carol Calderon, walks over to me, wiping her hands on a towel around her neck. Her nickname is Caro, and she's my best friend. She asks, "Ness, you staying to watch the players for a while?"

"Yes, I'm going to do my Government homework while I eyeball those jocks. No one's home at my house and I don't want to go and be alone... again."

"I hear that, but since I have three brothers, I'd kind of like being alone," she say with a sigh.

"You can come over on the weekend, we can have some girl time, and you can have testosterone free space," I suggest.

"Okay, I'll call you, I gotta go, my mom will skin me alive if I don't get home before she gets home from work. See you tomorrow." She waves as she skips away toward the student parking lot. I notice the guys behind her and can't look elsewhere for a few minutes before I start my homework. They're gorgeous. One of these days maybe one will like me, and we can be friends. Perhaps I can get a kiss for the first time. Oh crap, I'll probably suck at kissing.

I shake my head and pick up a pencil. I better quit ogling them and study, or I won't get anything done. Seems like only a few minutes and a deep voice brings me out of my concentrated focus on my studies.

"Hi, I'm Jimmy. You doin' homework?"

I peek at him through my lashes. Oh, man, he's so cute, and I've been crushing on him forever. Please let me be able to talk. This blue-eyed blond-haired babe makes me tingle in places I didn't know I had. I answer slowly, so I don't mess up. "I'm on page 367." Well, so much for not messing up. I roll my eyes before trying to regain my composure. "I mean, I'm studying for my Government test on Friday. That's the hardest class for me. My name is Vanessa Cutter. You can call me Ness or Nessa if you want."

He smiles at me and says, "I think I will, Ness. I'm good at Government would you like a study partner? I'm available."

Holy crap, yes! I take a breath letting it out slowly as I answer, "Yes, I would. I'll make you a sandwich if you want to study at my house."

"I don't know Ness, you live in the rich end of town, and my family doesn't have the best rep. Your parents won't want me there."

"What they don't know won't hurt them. They won't be home for a week. My parents are overseas for business. They'll be back before the Valentine's dance though, for my twin sisters' big after party. So you're welcome to come, like I said, what they don't know won't hurt them."

"It's a date then. Just let me shower, and I'll be back. If you're still here, I'll know you're still cool with me going home with you."

I nod and smile as he races off, I can't help but notice his tight ass in his practice uniform. They had to have made those that way for torture. I pack up my books and take them to my car. It's a beat-up Mustang, but I love it. On warm days, like today, I drive with the top down. My sisters have new cars, but I love mine. When I graduate, I plan on getting a job so I can get it painted and get new tuck and roll upholstery.

I mosey back to the bleachers and am texting Caro about Jimmy when Terry Counts walks up and says, "Hey baby, I see you waited for me."

"No, I'm waiting for a friend, and you aren't a friend, Terry." He's a jerk and always flirting and trying to get me to go out with him. Last year he threw me up against the lockers and kissed me. I refuse to think of that as my first kiss since I didn't participate and was mad at myself for not clocking him one. He likes to swat my butt if I pass him in the hall and I hate him for it every time. He leans in close to my face, and I back away from his bad breath. Several things are running through my mind but mostly ... I can kick him in the nards if he gets any closer.

Then a voice behind us says, "Hey Terry, keeping my girl company until I get here?"

The jerk backs off fast like he's been hit by a linebacker. Here's Jimmy to my rescue. He called me his girl. I'm going with it and stand, putting my arm around him as I say, "Hi handsome, took you forever."

We stroll away from Terry, his mouth gaping like a beached carp. When we get to my car and get inside, we turn toward each other and burst out laughing. We don't have to say a word, and I'm not apologizing. When I pull into the driveway at home, I pull around to the side of the house and pull out a car cover from a storage bin.

"I have to cover my car. Otherwise, Nina will have a heart attack if anyone sees it and complains that I need a new one. Some of our neighbors don't want an old car parked on this street. Nina refuses to let me have a new car, those are just for her darling daughters." I'm talking so fast I barely take a breath as I finish.

"Jimmy, my mother passed when I was a little girl, and my dad remarried. He does everything his wife tells him to, and I don't have much to do with either of them. Yeah, they feed me and pay the bills but nothing extra. Come on in, let's make a sandwich."

"I'd love that, little lady, I'm starving," he says and gives me his to-die-for grin.

This guy is so cute. I hope I can eat without looking like a total idiot. I lead the way into the house and explain, "This is the front room where my family has gatherings. I usually just pass right by. The kitchen is more my speed. I love to cook. If you want, I can cook us something better tomorrow after practice?"

"I'd love that. Ness, I need to say something, so you know about my family and me." His eyes are down, and he looks up at me with his brows knit. He's serious, and his cheeks are flushed.

I lower my voice a bit to soften it before saying, "Go ahead, it's okay. I'll listen with an open mind." Then I quickly look away to get the lunchmeat, cheese, and condiments. The whole grain wheat bread is already on the bar. I reach back into the fridge and get drinks.

"If you already know, just stop me, so I don't embarrass myself any more than I have to." He glances my way, and I nod that I will as he continues. "My mom passed when I was born and my dad ... well, he was known as the town drunk then. He lost everything he had worked for his whole life." He gulps, his Adam's apple bobbing, then adds, "In a drunken rage one night he proceeded to beat me black and blue. I was eleven, so I don't remember much. When the neighbors saw us in the front yard, they called the police. It was Mr. Cobb, our history teacher, he tried to calm my dad, but he was too far gone. When the cops showed up, he somehow wrestled a gun away from an officer and shot him on accident. The fact is, he was trying to shoot himself, and the gun went off before he had it aimed. He's in jail for murder and child abuse, among other things. If you don't want to hang with me, I understand. Everyone knows this town was on fire with the gossip for years."

"Oh, no, that sucks. I'm sorry you had to go through that, Jimmy. I didn't know, but my family is always part of the town gossip. I try to ignore it. Do you see your dad?"

"No, I tried to once, but he yelled at me and said he hates me and never come back, so I haven't. I just wrote him off. I think he wanted me to forget about him and move on."

"Wow, that's harsh. I don't see my parents much, and they prefer my half-sisters and Europe, but I don't think they hate me. Maybe, we can be the black sheep of our families together."

He laughs and says, "We're a pair. I think we're the white sheep though. At least I intend to be, and you seem to be pretty special."

"Why, thank you, Mr. Danforth. I'll take your praise," I say, flashing my best smile. I hand him a sandwich and open a bag of chips and put them between us to share. He takes a big bite and eats like he hasn't in a while. "Umm, do you mind if I ask? Where do you live? Do you have a foster family?"

He stops and takes a drink of soda pop. "Ness, I'm telling you all my secrets for a reason. I've wanted to ask you out for a long time now and finally took a chance today. Are you going to be my girl for real, or are we just friends before I spill my guts."

"Well, since you're asking. I kinda would like you to be my guy. I won't tell your secrets if you don't tell mine." I hope he likes me because I've been thinking about him forever.

A crazy hot grin spreads out on his face, and he says, "I won't tell your secrets. I don't have a foster family I'm eighteen and live where ever. I crash at Jaden Murphy's a lot, Joe Keet's, or wherever I can. Sometimes in the park, I can always get a shower in the locker room. It's not bad. I'm okay."

"Well, tomorrow, I'll be cooking for us. What do you want?" I think I better cook a lot to make sure he eats. "Do you have a job?"

"I deliver papers for the newspaper in the early mornings. It doesn't pay a lot but enough to keep me fed. Can you make spaghetti?"

"Sure can. Never worry about food again and save if you want to. You're my boyfriend, and what kinda girl would I be if I didn't make sure you were eating?"

"I won't turn down a good meal, but I'm okay, Ness. Thank you for the sandwich."

"Do you want more, or do you wanna watch a movie?"

"Movie if you'll talk to me too."

We spend the rest of the evening ignoring the movie and talking. We fall asleep on the couch, and he wakes me early to say goodbye. I make him a peanut butter sandwich to take and some coffee for breakfast. He kisses me on the cheek, the gleam in his eyes sets my stomach to flutter. I'm so happy!

2

SCHOOL DAYS

WHEN WE GET TO SCHOOL, THERE'S A BUZZ GOING AROUND. Caro walks up with a finger to her lips, and a follow me motion. I follow her to my locker, and I open it for privacy.

"So, spill the tea, you didn't call last night, and I left you alone about that hot jock Jimmy Danforth, but now I need the chisme." That's gossip a la Caro.

"Holy crap, Caro, isn't he a doll? He came over, and I made us sandwiches, we talked and talked. We turned on a movie and still talked and get this ... we fell asleep on the couch. He's my boyfriend now! I'm in freaking love!" We screech in glee and hug while jumping up and down.

"You better watch out, girlfriend. If your stepmom finds out you had a boy over she'll make you clean the pool again or something. And yeah, he's cute. I like his ass in his uniform."

I giggle at her comment before the bell rings for our five minutes get to class warning. We have to cross the whole campus, so I start at a fast clip turning back to yell, "See you at lunch."

"Simon, vata loca.," I reply with my favorite Spanish slang.

"Yeah, that's me, but you're just as crazy, girl." I wave, and we split off going to class.

I have Jimmy in my homeroom. But I won't see him after that until sports when the cheer squad is practicing, and he's with the football team. I'd never get any work done if I had him in more classes. I can't concentrate as it is. Mr. Cobb starts class, but I can tell something's up and wait wondering what it could be—when the ball drops.

Mr. Cobb says, "Students, I have an announcement. If you can't take some bad news about our little town, I ask you to leave the classroom and meet with Mrs. Singer in room 202." He pauses, and a few students actually get up and leave. Our school is structured, so we walk into each quad of classrooms from the outside. There are two levels in the main building that we navigate with stairs, but the other buildings are ground floor only.

Our history teacher closes the door after watching the students leave for Mrs. Singer's room. He continues, "I don't know if any of you know any park rangers or not, but last night there was a disturbance in town, and a Federal Park Ranger was killed. It happened during a robbery, and the officer was off duty. The officer's family has been notified, and the killer has been caught, but the Sheriff's office wants all residents to be on guard for suspicious activity. You need to be aware of your surroundings and be home early folks. They believe they have all the parties involved. To be safe, we want you to be especially careful in case others are working with the criminal."

I sit and try to absorb the news, but it's a shock. Mike George pipes up and asks, "Who was the officer, Mr. Cobb?"

His name was David Sean Ross, a ranger from the caverns. You'll probably see something on the news later. If you'd like to see your counselors feel free to leave class and go to room 202, they're in there at this time. No one moves, and the teacher assigns reading on chapter eighteen and says we'll have a quiz tomorrow. That gives me a day to study, but exams on Friday are usual. I kinda like it that way, so there isn't a lot of homework on game nights. The bell rings, and we head to our next class. I wait as Jimmy catches up to me, he says, "You want to sit with me at lunch, beautiful?"

My heart is beating a mile a minute as I say, "Yes, see you there."

LATER, I wander into the lunchroom, get a tray, and find Jimmy first thing. He pats the seat beside him. I notice Caro is there sitting at the same table, that's nice of him to include her. She's lapping up the attention from Jimmy's hunky friends Joe, Jaden, and Zane. My girl is too busy to pay much attention to me but pats me on the butt as I pass her on the way to sit by my new boyfriend. Whatever, we can talk later in the locker room before practice anyway.

After I shift my chair just a little closer to Jimmy's, we share my tray. Actually, I ate my fruit and Jimmy ate the rest. This might just work out for me because I never eat everything and feel guilty throwing a tray full of food away. It's quieter in here than usual, and an all-around more serious attitude today throughout the cafeteria.

Jimmy asks, "So, are you okay given the news about the park ranger?"

"I am, I didn't know Officer Ross, my family might. Did you know him?"

"No, but I'm sorry about what happened and all," he says.

About that time, Caro shifts in her chair, and it slides right out from under her. She's anything but graceful as her legs fly straight up. Several kids at the next table begin laughing loudly while making a show of pointing at her. I know she's gonna be embarrassed so I run around the table to help her up. Joe's there and helps her before I even get a hand out. She's looking at him like she wants to lick sugar off his lips. Cool, but I'm teasing her about it.

Jimmy picks up her chair, turning it over and says, "Would you look at this, one of the legs is bent, and the joint is creased. They really need to get some newer chairs, that could have been serious."

Mr. Winn, the lunchroom monitor, is just walking up and says,

"You couldn't be more right." He slides another chair to Caro and asks, "Are you alright, Miss Calderon?"

"Just my ego is damaged," she answers.

"If you have any trouble go see the nurse," the teacher says.

When she nods at him, he walks off and continues to monitor the room. There aren't fights here like in the lower grades, but it's always best we have a teacher on hand.

We all sit back down, and Zane says, "Do you think someone did that on purpose? It looks like it was bent recently, there's no rust."

My boy answers, "That's exactly what I thought, especially after the bullies next to us laughed so hard when Caro fell. Let's be on guard for stunts like this."

We've all seen Travis Blake, one of the kids who laughed and coincidentally a part of Terry's crew, do some awful things to others. The students here are always on guard for his unwanted pranks. He gets really creative sometimes. This prank could have really hurt someone, but we have no proof he's the instigator. We can be more vigilant like we were told this morning.

I change the subject after everyone pauses, "Hey, I have event planning in student council next. Do any of you have any ideas I can pitch for the Valentine's dance?"

Joe says, "Yeah, jeans and tees, no suits!"

"I think that might be great and Mrs. Singer will go for date clothes if I ask, but it's always a vote," I say, as the bell rings. Jimmy holds my hand as we leave the lunchroom, and it makes my heart swell.

His voice cracks as he asks, "Can I take you to the dance, Ness?" I'm so happy I could break out in a cheer. Instead, I giggle, hug him, then say, "Yes! And will you go to the after party at my house with me? My sisters are throwing this one and it'll be nice. All the kids are talking about it I'm sure you've heard already."

"Yes, if your parents say it's okay."

3

THE MALL

I HAVE A TERRIBLE HEADACHE, AND MY HANDS START TO SHAKE. My blood sugar is low. I pull a protein bar out of my bag and eat a couple of gummy bears. If I eat too many it only makes my blood sugar soar then drop even lower, then I'd get really cold, shaky, and go to sleep. So, I'm careful not to have too much sugar. I'm just finishing my little snack when Jimmy gets out of the locker room. He's heading toward me when Terry throws a water balloon at him hitting him in the eye as it bursts.

I rush over and push the asshat as hard as I can. "Oh, it's on, you punk ass bitch." One thing I learned by being a cheerleader is how to kick precisely where I want. Time for my kick-em in the balls move. Without even thinking, my hands go up along with my right leg straight into his crotch.

Wait, how'd I miss? Just then, I notice Jimmy has me around the waist, pulling me away from Terry. I'm screaming at him, "You fucking brat. You pussy! I'm calling security." I pull out my phone, but he laughs and takes off with his buddies who are attached to him at the hip.

Jimmy feels me relax and lets me go. I turn around to check on him, and he's standing there with a knuckled hand on his injured eye and sporting his amazing grin... staring at me.

"It's okay, Nessa, I don't think I'm hurt."

I raise my hands to his face and turn him toward me. There's a red splotch where the balloon hit. I move Jimmy's fist away from his eye and say, "Let me be the judge of that, handsome."

His eye is really red, but it's not bleeding. It's swollen but not shut. "Let's go home, and I'll make you an ice pack. You can sit with it while I start our dinner. I wonder what makes Terry and his goons do shit like this. He makes me so mad!"

He puts his hand back on his eye. "It's too bright to keep my eye open out here. Yeah, let's go. Damn that, Terry. I'm going to have to be sure he doesn't hurt others like this."

We get to my house, and my boy's already better just being inside out of the sun and the dry wind. We set our books on the table, and I kick off my shoes. I'd never get away with doing that if my stepmom was home. I get a pack of frozen peas out of the freezer and hand them to Jimmy. He accepts the makeshift ice pack and lays down on the sofa right off the kitchen. I start some music and wash my hands before starting our food.

"On second thought, I'm going to change. I'll be right back," I say, but he's already snoring softly. I watch him breathe for a second, his muscled chest moving up and down. After fantasizing briefly about how Jimmy would look without his shirt, I let out a soft moan and go change.

When I come back, the peas are on top of his head. I snort, that's so cute. I take them off and cover him with the throw on the back of the sofa. He snuggles into it and smiles. A ringing starts as I pass by the fridge, answering a video call on the fridge has got to be the weirdest thing.

"Hi, hun. How are things going? Nina told me to call and make sure you hadn't burned the house down."

"Hi, Dad. No, the house is fine, no fire. I was about to make something for dinner, though. Dad, I want to ask a boy to the after party the girls are planning. Is that okay?" I ask him before the wicked witch of the west finds out and forbids it.

"Well, that's okay, I guess. Anyone, we know?"

"I don't think, so he's one of the football players who asked me to the dance." On face value, he'll be happy it's a football player.

"Okay, just don't cause any trouble before we get home. You can use my credit card and find you a new outfit. Your sisters and Mom have shopped so much they have a whole new wardrobe, and their dresses for the party are very nice. Now, we're coming home on Sunday so make sure the house is clean and pay the gardener, so the yard looks nice and I don't get yelled at for the shape of the place, please."

"Thank you, Dad. I know just the outfit I want. And yes, I'll clean the whole house and talk to the gardener, but the yard looks good now. See you soon."

"I'll see you Sunday," he says and disconnects.

I stare pitifully into the blank screen and say dismally, "I love you and can't wait to see you, Vanessa, and you sure are pretty. Is that a new shade of lip gloss you have on?"

I start when Jimmy comes up behind me while I'm talking to myself. He says, "I was thinking the same thing. But hey, we're tough and have each other, right?" He puts his hand on my back, and I melt into him.

"Damn skippy, tough guy. Your eye looks much better. It's still red but better. How does it feel?"

"Scratchy, but yeah, better. How can I help?"

"Here." I hand him all the stuff to make the garlic bread. "You make the bread, and I'll finish the spaghetti. The salad is already finished. What kind of dressing do you like?"

"Anything will do, but I like ranch if you have it."

"You bet." I get it out and set it on the bar where we're going to eat. "You know I've been thinking about Terry and his goons. We really need to do something about him. They could hurt someone."

"Nessa, you're so cute. Most of the team is already trying something to see if it'll work. We have a plan to watch and interfere anytime we see them picking on someone. We've been making videos and stepping in. I'm pretty sure that's why he hit me with the balloon today. He's noticing. The football team and I text each other as soon as we see the bullies starting shit and pressure them to stop. That way there's no violence, and we try to stay in pairs. I wonder, maybe you and your friends could help us too?"

"I'd love that, and I'll ask them after dinner," I say.

He reaches for a knife at the same time I do and our hands touch. It gives me tingles. He gives me the knife and gets another. When we've finished cooking and eating we clean up, and I tell him about the shopping trip I have planned and my promise to make sure the house is spotless.

"I figured you had a maid for that, Ness. Would you like some help? I can come over after you're finished shopping if you like."

"That would be great, but you will have to be gone on Sunday when my dad gets home. Nina will have instant mad cow disease if I have company. And yeah, we do have a maid, but she's only here twice a week."

We go into the living room and pick another movie to ignore. I can't help myself and get caught staring at my new beau.

He smiles and says, "I'd like to kiss you. If it's alright with you?"

My head explodes, and I have no brains left. I nod and stare blankly.

He leans into me, and I don't know what to do. Do I turn my head? Which way? He takes over and does it all. With a gentle hand on my chin, he turns my face with the tenderest of pressure. I bet he can feel my heart, it's beating so hard. His lips meet mine... they are sweet and soft. I close my eyes. Oh, he's so perfect. My stomach flutters and I need to move but want more. He pulls away enough that I can stare into his eyes, and he can see into my soul.

I swallow hard, and my voice shakes as I sputter, "That was nice. Do you know that's my first real kiss?"

His eyes squint and crease with his smile, and he says, "I'm privileged. You want me to teach you to French kiss?"

"Is it hard?"

"No, and if you don't like it, just tell me to stop, and I will."

"Okay, then, show me."

He moves toward me again once more, touching my mouth with his. This time I feel his tongue on my lips, slowly his tongue runs over them. His gentle caress starts the tingle in my stomach again. I open my mouth. He moves his tongue on mine and opens his mouth wider. Bam! Electricity shoots right between my legs, and I roll over and sit on his lap. OMG, what am I doing?

He stops and looks to see if I'm okay. I know that he's surprised but happy that I climbed onto his lap. I laugh and hop back onto my own seat. When I do, I notice the bulge in his pants. The euphoria I feel knowing I did that to him is indescribable. The wetness I feel from between my legs isn't lost on me either.

We finish our dinner and spend the rest of the night talking. Once again, we fall asleep together wrapped in each other's arms, but this time it's on purpose. When he wakes me in the morning, I send him off with another peanut butter sandwich and coffee. I'm walking on air as I shower for my shopping trip. I call Caro and see if she can go with me.

She says, "I'll meet you there. You have cheese. I can tell by your tone. I'll be there as soon as the mall opens."

"Will do, see you at nine in front of Macy's."

We pick out the cutest outfits. Mine is a turquoise top that shows my midriff and a jean pencil skirt with a matching turquoise and pink intertwined heart. Jimmy said his favorite color is turquoise and this is perfect since mine is pink. I top it all off with a black leather jacket. I figure I'll need it since there's a cold front coming in. Even if it doesn't turn cold, the warm weather we have isn't going to last. In any case, who can't use a leather jacket? It hardly ever snows in Cueva Hallow, so I'm not worried on that front.

Caro gets a similar outfit but with ripped skinny jeans and a plaid over shirt in red and black. We text the squad to meet us in the mall's food court to eat and show them our clothes.

"That is slammin', Ness. I love yours too, Caro. When I get my outfit, I'll make sure it's close but different," says Killer who showed up with our other friends and is sitting drinking a soda. Her nickname is a mix of her first name Katy and her last Diller. She likes it, but she looks more like the girl next door with her soft brown hair and baby blues than a moody emo type you imagine would belong to the name.

"Yes, and no one get too matchy-matchy, tell your dates what color and maybe they can coordinate a tee or something with you," I say. "I have to go, but I'll see you on Monday. If you want to buy a pin that looks like lips or a heart before the dance Friday, make sure and bring money they're five dollars each.

"Ness, do we order them from you or Mrs. Singer?" Supe, our other friend who came with Killer asks. Her name is pronounced 'soup.' We didn't have to give Supe a nickname because her name was cool, to begin with. It means, 'I knew' in Spanish. Her mother is from Spain. That's where her father and mother met and married. Supe is as beautiful as her mom with blond curls and golden eyes.

"I'll send you all a link, you can give Mrs. Singer cash or pay online," I reply.

Killer asks, "Does everyone have a date, or does someone want to go with me?"

Candice, also known as Dice, says, "I don't, I'll go with you Killer if you pick me up. What about the rest of you, do we make it a threesome or a quartet? We can add you too, Ness."

"No, I have a date with Jimmy Danforth," I say with a grin.

"Holy shit! That's great girl how did you do that? Damn, he's hotter than a stolen tamale!" Supe asks.

I laugh at her description. "I don't know, but I'm happy and yeah he's finer than powdered sugar and twice as sweet! He kissed me last night," I spill.

The girls are excited and want details. I tell a little but not all. No way do I want them fawning over my guy. He's mine. I dig in my pocket for my keys and give my girls a hug then say, "I have to get home. Bye y'all. I don't want to face the wrath of the step-monster if she finds the house less than perfect."

4

PASTA ON US

THE WHOLE HOUSE IS GLEAMING AND SMELLS LIKE ORANGE cleaner. Jimmy and I are taking one last tour to be sure everything is perfect. We decide to go out to dinner and not mess the kitchen up. Jackets on, I add a hat and scarf, and we head to my car and uncover it. The cover is crispy from the cold. I wrestled with the thing, trying to fold it in the gusty wind. Jimmy takes it and makes it look easy, then he puts it away in the cubby.

"Looks like the front is here. I hate the wind. Do you have a place to stay tonight, Jimmy? My parents will kill me if they find you here in the morning. On second thought if you stay in the pool house and sneak out..."

"No, Nessa, I'm staying with Jaden tonight. I don't want to take any chances. Your parents will have me arrested if they catch me. Just being in your neighborhood has people watching me like I'm a dang cat burglar. I told your neighbors that I was helping with yard work yesterday."

"Oh, did the Sims talk to you?" I ask, pulling out of the drive.

"Yes, is that the guy's name? He asked if he could help me and what was I doing there since the Cutters are out of town. Then he proceeded to tell me they don't need anyone who looks suspicious in the neighborhood. That's when I came up with the yard work story."

"Thanks, that was good thinking on your part. They could tell my parents then I'd never see you again." No, I won't let that happen. I'll fight them if they try that.

"The Pasta Joint is just a few blocks away. Do you want pasta again? They have other stuff if you don't," I ask.

"I love pasta, so I'm fine with that. I'm not picky," he answers, getting into the passenger side. I start off and can feel the gusts of wind pushing the car at times.

When we pull into the parking lot, I get ready to get out. I stop to let a pretty lady heading to the restaurant's door cross in front of us first. A big puff of wind hits her, and her dress blows up over her head. We're flashed black panties with the hashtag 'Wantsome' written on her backside. I can't help but snort and try not to laugh. When she wrestles her dress down, she has to stand there holding it, so it doesn't blow right back up. Jimmy hurries over and opens the door for her. He's so great!

I walk in after her, and she has that damn lace from her skirt stuck on a metal buckle on the back of her jacket. Every time she shifts, she flashes the hashtag. I walk over and put my hand at her waist, pulling it loose and dropping it as I say, "Wow, you look so nice in that outfit. I can't believe it is so windy all of a sudden."

She smiles and says, "Thank you, I wouldn't have even worn this to work if I'd have known it was going to be this bad out. Have a nice meal, young lady. That's a nice gentleman you got there."

We seat ourselves, then our waitress comes over and takes our drink orders. She smiles flirtatiously at Jimmy asking him for his order, then while never looking at me, she asks, "And you, what would you like?"

I say, "I want strawberry lemonade hot, please."

She stares at my boy again, "Is that all, or would you like bread to start?"

He smiles back at her and answers, "Yes, bread would be nice."

She replies, "You got it, sweetie." As she turns, she scrapes a finger across Jimmy's shoulder, then walks away.

As she walks off, I huff, "What a flirt!"

Jimmy says, "Hmm? What are you getting? I haven't been here before."

"I like everything, but the linguine alfredo with green chile and chicken is wonderful."

"Okay, then that's what I want. Ness, I need to know what to wear to the Valentine's dance. And what about the party at your house later, do you really think I should show up?"

"Yes, you're my boyfriend, the first one I've ever had, and I want you there. I got an outfit for the dance that will match your turquoise tee and your black leather jacket. My outfit has pink on it too but other than that its pretty date night looking. Casual, but nice."

"That sounds like something I can do," he agrees just as our waitress brings our drinks. Now that I think about it, I'm sure she's just *his* waitress. However, she did bring my hot lemonade and the bread. She also set down a plate of spices then pours virgin olive oil on it before she takes our orders watching him the whole time.

Jimmy looks at the spices and oil, then me with a questioning glance. I pull apart the bread and break off a piece and dip it then eat it. He smiles and copies me. We tear off hunks of the hot bread and dip it into the spicy oil talking until our food arrives.

By the time we are done, Jimmy has eaten all of his and half of mine that I wasn't going to eat. Then that pesky waitress comes over, on her way to another table and asks, "Would you like some dessert?" I'm just about to tell her no when Mrs. Hashtag hurries past our table to answer the phone and runs straight into our flirt... I mean, waitress. A full bowl of ravioli pours on Jimmy's head. One overly plump square seems to be losing its grip on the top of his head. Jimmy sits frozen as it slowly slides down his forehead and off his nose before plopping onto the floor with a splat.

The room seems to have gone completely silent. All eyes are on us waiting on the explosion of anger. I can only stare at my marinara covered boyfriend. I blink, then he blinks, then we grin at the same moment. I sputter out, and he starts cackling too. The silence in the room is replaced with more laughter, the waitress apologizing, and Mrs. Hashtag is a frozen statue unable to comprehend what she'd caused. She collects herself while the phone continues to ring and says, "I'm so sorry. Let me pay for your meals and give you a gift card for your next trip."

She's so devastated that I say, "Thank you, but really we're okay. At least I am. This is my boyfriend, Jimmy. You're all right, aren't you?" I ask blinking and holding back more mirth.

"I'm all right. Where is the men's shower?" he deadpans.

After she tells him where the men's room is, she has the mess cleaned up in minutes with the waitress's help. When Jimmy comes back, he's as clean as he can get but has a big splotch of the red marinara staining his tee front. Mrs. Hashtag gingerly walks over to us with a card in her hand. The lady chokes out that she's the manager and apologizes several times and gives us a fifty-dollar gift card. After my football player assures her he's okay we leave.

Getting in the car, I ask, "So, do you want to go to my house and get a shower, or can you shower at Jaden's?"

"Drop me off at Jaden's, beautiful, they're used to me there and won't care at all."

That's just what I do and miss him like crazy within minutes of dropping him off. His goodbye kiss tingles on my lips. I pull into my spot and cover my wreck before I go inside to dream about the best date ever.

5

THEY RETURN

I WAKE THE NEXT MORNING TO THE CHAOTIC SOUNDS OF MY family returning. I'm glad they're home and jump out of bed and dress quickly. In the bathroom, I rush then notice I look a little messy and brush my hair up into a bun not too messy and brush my teeth. Then run to meet them.

"Oh, good Lord, will you look at that. The dead have awakened, finally." She pauses long enough after 'awaken' that I thought she was done, and I start to smile at my sisters. Then the old bat snappishly continues on, "Vanessa, get this luggage and take it to our rooms. My head is killing me from jet lag. Did you hear me? Put the luggage in our rooms, and while you are there, unpack," my dad's wife orders.

If I pause any longer, she'll start screeching, and no one wants to hear that. Plus, my ears can't take her high pitched shrill this early in the day. My half-sisters don't suffer from the same demon malady as their mother. They come and give me welcoming hugs. Cess, which is short for Cecily, says in my ear, "I'll get mine and Cilla's."

Cilla is short for Cecilia. Cess knows her mother is hard on me and tries to make up for it when she can. Cilla never tries. We love her, but she's a brat. Not a mean brat just spoiled and doesn't think of others often.

My sisters are twins and real beauties. They're everything I'm not. blond, blue eyes, tall, and pretty. When they were born, I was kept away from them and not allowed to touch unless we had family pictures, and even then, it was strained. As they grew, we found ways that we could interact without getting into trouble. They're two years younger than me but were accelerated a grade because Nina forced the issue. I think they could've made it without her and her donations because they're smart. That isn't how it happened, though, we love each other but aren't very close.

Nina leaves with a glare my direction. I grab the luggage and take off to her room. She has a separate one from Dad. Where is he, anyway? I put everything away. I've been doing the laundry since I was fourteen, so I know where everything goes. Nina says she saves on the cost of the service if they only have dry cleaning and stuff she thinks I'll ruin cleaned. After everything is put away, I take Dad's suitcase and go to his room. I just barge in without knocking since he isn't here and catch him and Nina in an embrace. They both turn, and she yells, "Get out! Vanessa, you need to learn some manners. It's common courtesy to knock on a closed door."

My dad just stands there and lets her yell. I drop his suitcase and run out. Tears run down my face. It was too much to think they might have missed me. I knew it would be this way and foolishly got my hopes up. As for Dad defending me, yeah, that never happens either. I run to my room to grab a jacket and my phone. Then I'm out the back door as fast as I can make it. I get into my car, start it, and pull out of the drive. When I'm at the end of the driveway, Nina is screaming at me to get back here I have work to do and didn't ask if I could leave. I pretend I didn't see her and keep going. I'll probably have to pay for that, but just this minute I really don't care. I stop in an alley around the corner and take out my phone to call Jimmy. He answers on the first ring. His pleasant voice making me feel better. He says, "Hey gorgeous, what's up? Is your family home yet?"

I blubber what happened to him, and he can't understand a word I say.

"Hang on just a bit, sweetheart. Where are you? I'll come to you?"

"No, I'll come to you. Where are you?"

"Jaden's dad took us to the diner for breakfast. They're leaving, but I'll tell them I can make my own way to practice today. It doesn't start until ten, so we have a couple of hours."

I say, "I'll be right there, bye."

When I get to the diner, there's my boy waiting for me in a booth. The joy of seeing someone who cares, after leaving a house where I'm treated like the hired help, pushes my emotional rollercoaster over the edge. I'm quickly blubbering again. No one ever waits for me. I pause and wipe away my tears with the bottom of my tee, then walk up to him. He reaches out for me and pulls me to him. He can tell this morning has been hard on me. I let the tears leak out again, but this time, I'm quiet about it. When I've cried all I'm going to, I scoot away and grab some napkins and blow my nose then wipe my face. I should get up and go wash it off, but I don't want to leave him yet.

I sniff and say, "Sorry, about that. I'm not used to someone caring, and I just broke down. I usually don't cry. You're a bad influence." I chuckle, so he knows I'm joking. He's the best thing to ever happen to me.

"I'm not worried about it, Nessa. I'm here for you twenty-four-seven. Now, can you tell me what happened and why you aren't home with your family?"

"It's the step-monster. She hates me. I was ordered to put away the luggage and the clothes for them. I thought they were in the living room, and my dad wasn't even there. When I started to put my dad's stuff away. I didn't knock on the door I just went in and caught him kissing Nina. She yelled at me for not having better manners. Yeah, I deserved it because I didn't knock."

"What, why can't she put up her own stuff? And no, most kids do that to their parents. But most parents love their kids and laugh or talk to them in private. Hell, some of the guys have told whoppers about their parents, and you're the only one I've ever heard of in trouble. You don't deserve abuse, Ness."

"You think yelling is abuse? I just wanted them to miss me a little. I think that's what affected me."

"Yes, I know people yell but Ness that was too much. She made you feel like a maid that doesn't belong in the family. No one should be made to feel so small."

"I guess I don't really understand it that way. I do understand you care for me, and it makes me happy. Thank you for being here for me." My phone rings, and it's my dad. I carefully pick it up and glance at Jimmy he nods so I answer.

"Vanessa, where are you? Your mother is flaming mad, and I'm not happy either. Get home now, or you will be grounded longer than you already are." He hangs up without letting me tell my side.

"I have to go face the music. If I don't, I won't be able to go to the dance."

"Do I need to go with you to be sure you're okay?"

"No, I'll text later if they don't take my phone away. If they do, I'll use my computer."

"Are you sure? I don't mind what they do to me."

"I care. It'll only make things worse. I think I should order some lattes. Maybe that'll soften the blow."

Jimmy waves over a waitress named Lou and I order them to go. It is only minutes, and I'm out the door on my way back to the place I live. I can't really think of it as a home. Not with that woman there.

6

MY PUNISHMENT

I'm numb on the way home. I do have feelings, but they've been dulled by my stepmother's harassment, especially after her performance today. Since storming out, I need to find some way of not being grounded for life. There's only one thing I can think of to do, and that is apologizing, and I will.

After parking, I set the coffees on the bin that holds the car cover, take it out, and cover my car. When I head into the house with the lattes, I take a deep breath hoping the coffees help a little. My dad is waiting in the foyer with a scowl.

He says, "I'm glad you can do what you're told sometimes, Vanessa. Your mother is in her bedroom, crying her eyes out over your behavior. What do you have to say for yourself."

My anger flares. If I weren't so mad, I'd probably be thankful he is letting me speak. I blurt, "First off, she isn't my mother and has never even pretended she likes me. So just forget me feeling sorry for her crying. Second, you weren't home and didn't even greet me like you missed me, much less her. I didn't know you were here when she ordered me to put up the luggage and everyone's clothes. Which I did without complaining. Third, I'm sorry I walked in on you, but I had no idea you were here. I do apologize for that. I should have knocked."

My dad glares and says, "I should have known you would be the hard kid. Nina always tells me what a test you are. You have chores just like everyone else, and it isn't going to kill you to do some work around here. You're grounded until I say you aren't. Now, give me your phone."

"What? No, Dad, the Valentine's Day dance is next weekend. I'm part of the committee. I have cheerleading every day that I can't miss and student council. I just met a boy I like and wanted you to meet him. Please, don't do this. I'll do extra chores."

"Don't tell me what to do little miss. What... oh yes, a boy? Who?"

Uh oh, I should've kept that quiet for now. Me and my big mouth. I hear an acid tone behind my dad.

Nina spits, "Hand your dad your phone you little bitch. Your apology is worthless. We come home to your attitude, and this house stinks and is filthy. You get in that front bathroom and clean it until it sparkles."

I take my phone and hand it to my dad. He isn't so upset now that he sees a little of mad Nina. I head to my room and take off my jacket and get my cleaning clothes on then go the front bath. I've decided from now on I'll call Dad, Jacob. He isn't a father figure to me anyway. I stop in the hallway when I hear Jacob and Nina arguing.

"Nina, I know that you have tried to raise Vanessa as your own and treat her the same as the twins, but you will never call my daughter a bitch again. Do you hear me?"

"I'm so sorry." She's crying again. "I was just so mad. She is the worst child, and I lost it. I'll tell her I'm sorry about that and you can give her back her phone in a few days instead of a month. Okay, Pookie? Do you forgive me?"

"Yes, dear...,"

I suck in air so fast, and they turn to see me staring at them, slack-jawed, from the hallway. Nina grimaces and slams the door. I go and clean the already clean bathroom again. It smells good to me. I'm not sure what she thinks smells terrible. Maybe it's the air-freshener plug-in. I take it out of the gold socket and sniff it. Well, it is a little strong, so I wrap it in a plastic bag and with intentions of taking it to the dumpster. I wheel around. There is Nina standing watching me.

"Don't think I'm going to be easy on you now, you little bitch. Go to your room. I don't want to see your face for the rest of the day."

Glaring unswervingly into her hateful eyes, I nod and quickly spin on my heel, leaving the back of my head only a few inches from her stooped over face. I take the trash with me and go straight to my room and my computer. There's no way they're going to make me stay home from the dance and hell will freeze over before I tell them Jimmy's name. I'll just leave the party and meet him under the bridge while they have the after party for the twins. They'll never notice I'm not there. They never do. This time it should work to my advantage. I type out a message for Jimmy and send it with a heart emoji.

JIMMY: Are you okay? I'm worried?

Me: I will be, but I'm grounded, and they took my phone. The step-monster called me a bitch in front of my dad. That's never happened. She usually saves the really hateful jibes for when he isn't here.

Jimmy: When do you turn eighteen?

Me:? 3/17

Jimmy: I'll figure out something for us. So, you don't have to stay there after your birthday.

Me: I'd love that!

WE MESSAGE FOR A WHILE. When we stop, I pull out my homework and review it, making sure I have everything correct. After checking all of my homework, I put my pj's on and start to read an entertaining book about a group of teens in New York who solve ghost troubles. I like it because the main character is a girl my age. Plus, she has four boyfriends. What girl wouldn't want four dreamboats, but I'm more than happy with my one Jimmy.

I'm afraid to go get dinner since the step-monster said she doesn't want to see me. It isn't going to kill me to skip a meal anyway, so I read until I fall asleep. I'll leave early tomorrow, so I don't have to see her in the morning, and she doesn't give me more punishment. My punishment is really just being alive. Jimmy gives me hope there is something better.

7

I WAS HELPED

THE NEXT MORNING, I CAN'T GET OUT OF HERE FAST ENOUGH. I tiptoe out of my room and run smack into my... Jacob.

He hands me my phone and says, "I'm sorry we were so rough, but you're still grounded." He turns and leaves.

I whisper, "Have a good day, and do you have lunch money and gas?" It never happens, but it would be nice to hear him care.

IT IS cold and icy today. It's typical New Mexico, want different weather wait, and you can have all four seasons in a few days. When I get to the school parking lot, my tires skid a few feet on the icy pavement when I turn into the lot. It's on a slope, so I crank my tires around to make sure my car stays in place. If someone does bump it maybe it won't go too far. My thinking is probably not right. I should ask Jimmy if that would really work. I bet he knows.

When I get to the main building, Caro is walking toward me. She says, "What happened yesterday I know your family came home, but you didn't call."

"Oh yeah they're home, did you see the twins yet? It was terrible, and I'm grounded again. I'll be glad when I can just get out of there and have my freedom. I better start looking for a job."

"Are you kidding me? Never mind, forget I asked. That always seems to happen to you. Why should I think it would change? Yes, I saw those spoiled brats. They're wearing new clothes and sporting some very nice shoes too. What did you get?"

"Nothing..."

"Yeah, that's not different, either."

"It's okay Caro. The old bat would probably get me something horrid, so I don't look as good as her precious girls. I'm stopping here. I love my half-sisters; they aren't the problem."

Jimmy arrives just as we're walking to homeroom and says, "Hi ladies." Then he takes my hand and walks with me.

Caro winks and says, "Text when you can, I'll see you in athletics later."

When we get to class, my stomach growls and Jimmy takes a protein bar out of his jacket and hands it to me. I have coffee in my water bottle, so I have all the major food groups now including the sugar, but that's all my boy.

The whole day goes by pretty quick, and I'm excited to go to the student council event planning class before cheer practice and don't notice Terry, the bully, until he runs into me and backs me against the wall of the side of the building. I shout, but no one is near enough to hear us. A cold sweat break out on my body and I start to shake. The look on his face says it all, and it's not good.

With his hand on my mouth and his body pressing me hard to the wall, he says, "Keep your mouth shut Cutter, and I might not make you bleed too bad."

I test my legs and can move them, so I try to kick at him to get away, but he is too strong and shoves me to the ground holding me still with his legs. I squirm and bite his hand. He takes it, then slaps me hard. Wow, that hurts more than I thought it would. It rings my bell. I blink my eyes looking through a fog and shake my head. He grins at my reaction and hits me again, this time with his fist. I try to get away by bucking him off my hips. I'm unsuccessful. He loves the motion and says, "Oh, so you like it rough, do you?" He draws back to hit me again, but the punch doesn't land.

I didn't see what or who, but someone jerks him up, completely off the ground, and I pass out. I wake up in the nurse's office with a cold compress on my forehead. The nurse, Mrs. Sanders asks, "Miss Cutter, can you tell me what day it is?"

I groan, "Monday, Mrs. Sanders, it's Monday."

"How do you feel you have some scratches on your arms and your face is battered and bruised. I don't see any more damage. Is there more, and can you tell me what happened?"

"No, I was walking to Event Planning, and Terry Counts attacked me. I tried to get away, but he was too strong for me. He slapped me, then punched me. I was foggy from the hit and don't know what happened next, but I think someone saved me. That's all I remember."

"Security is here and needs to take your statement. Are you able to give them one? You can always stop if it's too much for you. Your sister Cecily is here, do you want to see her?"

"Yes, I think I can, and please bring my sister back."

Cess comes with a worried glance, hugs me, and asks, "Ness, are you okay? They're arresting that jerk!"

I hug her then say, "I'm not even sure of everything, but Terry attacked me, and someone helped me. Do you know who helped me? I didn't see them, but I'm sure they got me here."

"No, there is no one. They say that you fought Terry off by yourself and passed out in front of the nurse's office where she found you."

"That's so strange. I don't remember that."

Cess says, "I'll drive you home. Cilla already left in my car since I drove us this morning. She was afraid to drive with the roads so frosty. Oh, here's the officer, do you want me to stay with you?"

"Yes, stay."

"Miss Cutter, I'm Officer Jones, are you able to give me a statement?" We have several security guards, and he's the oldest of them in his forties. He has dark hair with just a shot of gray at the temples. He's still very fit and a tall man who we've all talked to at one time or another.

"Yes, sir, I believe so," I repeat everything I had told the nurse, and the officer writes it in his tablet as he records me.

After we're able to leave, Cess helps me walk out of the little room into the main part of the office, and Jimmy is waiting. He gets up and rushes to me and softly hugs me.

"I was so worried, Ness. What do you want me to do? I'll do whatever you want even go home with you to watch over you, so you aren't scared. That asswipe is arrested so he can't get you, but if you need me, I'll be there."

Cess says, "No, Jimmy, Nessa will call you later. If my mom sees you, she'll cause us all trouble. It's bad enough at home right now. I promise I'll call you if she can't."

I nod, and my head throbs from the motion. I say, "You are so cute. I'm all right. I will call, don't worry. Cess is driving me home. Are you staying with Jaden tonight?"

"Yes, don't worry about me. Cecily just take care of my girl and Ness if you can't come to school tomorrow, please let me know."

I kiss him on the cheek, and we all walk toward the parking lot where he helps me buckle up. I say, "Stop I'm not crippled just tired and want to rest. I'll text in a little while."

When I get home, Nina is waiting and questions me. She says, "Were you teasing this boy to make him come after you. You know that can get you hurt Vanessa?"

Cess says, "No, Mom, that isn't what happened. She was attacked. I'm taking her to her room. Since she wasn't allowed to eat last night, please make sure she gets a tray, the cook is here today, right?"

Jacob says from behind us, "What? Vanessa wasn't allowed to eat last night? You said she refused."

When did he get here? My mind must be a real mess because I don't know what is happening around me at all today.

Nina answers, "That must have been a misunderstanding. That's all, darling. Vanessa go to your room. I'll be sure you get a tray later. Cess, go get your sister and make sure she isn't worried about this fiasco."

Cess ignores her mom and walks with me to my room. I lay down, and she sits on the bed with me then says, "Ness, I'm so sorry she's so mean to you. I'll do better at intervening when I know you're going to have to pay for something she's angry about. Do you think maybe your grandparents would let you live with them if it gets worse?"

"Yes, I think that might be a good idea. I'll bring it up in the next few days." My voice trails off, I need to rest.

Cess leaves me with a hug, and I pull my body pillow tight. I'm asleep in no time and don't wake until the cook taps on my door. "Miss Cutter, I have your dinner. May I come in?"

I drowsily offer a, "Sure, come on in." I don't say anything else to her except, "Thank you," as she leaves. If we get too friendly with the help Nina fires them, so we pretty much don't do that anymore. I sit at my work table and eat and text Jimmy and Caro. My phone blows up and everyone on the cheer squad asks if I'm okay. Tween is so smart she made a chat with all of us, so I just use that one to answer everyone. I didn't tell everyone else that I think some unknown person helped me... but I do tell Jimmy.

He says he believes me and get some rest. Now that I'm full, that's all I want to do anyway. I can catch everyone up in the morning. I better take my tray to the kitchen or face another irate flare up from Nina. On my way, I overhear Jacob and Nina arguing again, but my brain's still in a fog, and I'm not interested in knowing what this one's about.

8

NO TOLERANCE

I CAN'T GET OVER HOW BRUISED UP MY FACE IS, AND ALL THE makeup in the world isn't covering them. I don't think it matters as much as my need for breakfast. The smell of waffles and bacon coming from the kitchen are lovely. I hurry to see if I can snag something without Nina noticing me. Maybe I can leave for school without getting waylaid by her... again.

I'm cold today, but the thermostat is set on seventy that means it can't be that cold in here, at least in my thinking. Maybe if I eat, it'll warm me up. I sneak into the kitchen and find like usual I'm the only family member here. I sit to eat a plate of waffles the cook just finished. I load them with fresh strawberries and whip cream. The crunch on the outside and the almost cake-like inside is incredible. These are the best waffles I've ever eaten.

I hear the others in the dining room, so I know they're also enjoying this wonderful treat too. Although, I can't really imagine Nina enjoying anything that I would. I finish my breakfast and scrape my plate. Wonder if I could get away with licking it clean... nah, bad idea. Nina might rip my ear off if I tried that. The coffee is ready, and I fill my thermal cup, leaving just enough room for creamer. I like my morning drink sweeter than most and add extra creamer. It's peppermint mocha, my favorite. I put my dishes into the sink and begin rinsing when the cook touches my arm and gently shakes her head side to side at me. She gently moves me aside, finishes rinsing and placing them in the dishwasher. I give her my best grateful smile and leave through the back door.

The parking lot at school is full of kids standing around, talking in the warm sunshine. As cold as it's been the last couple of days, the warming we have today is a welcome change. I find Jimmy up ahead. Beautiful weather, Jimmy nearby... yep, today is going to be a nice day. Jimmy spots me and along with several of his friends walks over. He kisses me lightly on my lips. My legs quiver.

"How're you feeling, Ness?" Jimmy asks.

He doesn't say I look terrible so I'm not going to worry about my bruises showing and answer, "My headache is mostly gone, but my jaw hurts, and my body is sore. All in all, I feel pretty good, especially with you here. I've been wondering... Jimmy, what can we do if this happens again?"

"Well, that's something that the guys and I have been talking about. We want to discuss it more at lunch, but we think it's a good idea if everyone walks in pairs the way we've been trying. And you, my little fighter, I don't want you walking around alone at all. Tell your sisters and friends the same thing, and maybe as a group, we can figure out something better."

"That's so sweet, Jimmy. Even my parents don't think like that about me."

"You want me to go tell them off? Maybe I can give Nina a wedgie?" He chuckles.

"No, silly," I say. "I can spread your message through. I missed student council yesterday, but I can talk to them today, and we can call a school-wide meeting. What do you think?"

All the boys bob their heads up and down in agreement.

Jimmy says, "Okay guys, I'll see you after homeroom. I'll be with

Vanessa if y'all will walk behind other students who are alone, I'd appreciate it. You don't have to be obvious."

With waves and goodbyes the others disperse.

Jimmy takes my hand in his and asks, "How did it go at home. Did things get better since you were hurt?"

"Not really, but Cess had a great idea. I think I should tell my parents I want to go stay with my grandparents on my mom's side. At least until I'm able to make it on my own. Nina half accused me of goading Terry into the attack. That isn't what happened, but she's always ready to see the worst or assume it about me."

"That bitch. I agree you've got move out, and your grandparent's house seems like the best answer."

"I think so. Then we'll be able to date in public at least." I smile then grimace as it pulls at my bruised face. He opens the door to our class, and we settle down to study.

Mr. Cobb says, "There will be a mandatory meeting in the gym after B lunch at 1:00 p.m. Security wants to review what to do if you're attacked and how to handle bullies."

I look at Jimmy and whisper, "Well, that takes care of that." Now that I don't have to worry about convening a student council meeting, we can think more about our plans for the dance."

The bell rings at the end of class, and we shuffle out with the rest of the kids. Jimmy goes his way, and I go mine, forgetting we'd decided to always walk with a partner.

One of Terry's friends is coming my way. I panic and speed up. He catches up, trips me as he rushes past, turns and says, "Fucking tease. Can't stay on your feet? You deserve to die for what you're doing to Terry. Why don't you do us all a favor and just kill yourself?" He leaves before I can get up, blending into the crowd.

Tween is helping me up when she says, "Did Travis just threaten you? No, I heard him. What should we do?"

"I think I should go to the office and report what just happened. Do you want to come and be my witness?"

"Yes, let's go," Tween urges.

The glass doors to the office open and my counselor Mr. Durham asks, "Is there a problem girls?"

Tween answers, "There is Mr. Durham. Ness was going to her next class, and Travis Parks tripped her. Then said she deserves to die for what she's doing to Terry Counts. He followed that up by asking her why she doesn't just kill herself. I was there and heard him. I walked her here to be a witness."

"Girls, please have a seat in my office."

When Mr. Durham is seated, he says, "You ladies know that these are serious charges." It isn't a question. "I'll have to have security here to take your statements? Also, I don't have to remind you, this room always has a camera running, and whatever is said here will be taped, or do I?"

"No, sir, we understand," I say.

Tween repeats that she understands also, and Mr. Durham calls security. Officer Brian White shows up to take our statements. He's shorter than Officer Jones and a lot younger. His short sandy hair is cut in a military style cut, and he's more severe than the other guards but we still all know him. When he enters the office, we're drinking water and talking to Mr. Durham more relaxed.

"Hello," Officer White says, looking at us before he shakes Mr. Durham's hand. "I understand you have something you want to report ladies. Is that correct?"

"Yes, sir, we have an issue concerning bullying and a threat," I answer. Tween nods, her curls bouncing.

"Alright then, by procedure, I'm required to get a written statement. Do you mind typing in what happened here?" He hands us a keyboard and turns a monitor toward us after opening a form.

We shake our heads, and the questions begin. We both type in our complaints and sign them electronically. "Because Travis said you deserve to die and not that he is going to kill you, it comes down to whether or not you believe he will come after you," Officer Brian says.

"No, I think he's just being mean and trying to defend his friend.

I can't say I'm not afraid, though. I am, but I don't think he'll kill me either. It would be nice if I didn't have to worry about the bullies, but that's the way it is."

"Well, we don't want that either. You must report it every time Miss Cutter and Miss Garcia. Is there anything else you want to tell me, or are we finished here?"

"I'm finished," I say.

Mr. Durham says, "Now girls get to your classes. He hands us permission slips, and he adds, "Don't walk alone, in fact, try to walk with several friends and listen to the officers later at the security meeting after lunch. They have some valuable information to share."

THE NEXT TIME I see Jimmy he's sitting beside me at lunch. I ask, "Did you hear what Travis did?"

"No, what happened?" The middle of his brow has three straight lines now, suspecting something terrible happened.

"He tripped me as soon as you were out of sight after homeroom. Then he told me I deserve to die for what I'm doing to Terry, and I should just kill myself." Uh oh, this isn't good. My boyfriend just went perfectly still. Without warning, he shoots up and calls to Joe and Jaden.

"Guys, Travis Parks tripped Ness and threatened her."

I hurry and stand between them and ask quickly, "Please, sit down and let's talk about this. I'm okay."

Jaden pipes up, "That kid's about as useless as a rubber nail."

Joe replies to me, "Yeah, let's plan first, then we'll take care of business."

I say, "No! No taking care of business. I already talked to my counselor and reported it to security. Don't do anything rash and get yourselves into trouble. I'm a big girl, and if I need help, I'll ask. For now, it's okay."

The boys sit, and we brush up on our plan to walk with a partner.

It's harder than we thought. Jimmy writes out a list of all of our classes and starts assigning football players and cheerleaders to each other. He stresses that we're the leaders of our class and if we see someone being bullied we need to get creative by shouting or joking with the bullies maybe. We can call each other and always have our phones ready to record.

The mood lightens up, and when the bell rings, we head to the gym for the mandatory meeting of all students. They hand us cards and a form at the doors. Jimmy's putting his in his pocket as he sits on one of the bleachers. I sit close to him, making sure as much of me as I can is touching him. Our friends squeeze into the rows around us.

Officer Brian is one of the security team giving the talk. The card they gave us has a number for the school superintendents and a national hotline number for students' rights if we feel the school isn't doing enough to protect us. It also has a number for suicide prevention. I'm getting frustrated because most of us understand that no one will use the hotlines, and if they do, nothing will be done. The security officers ask if there's anything we'd like to ask.

I can't hold myself back anymore and say, "Sir, we think that you are trying to be nice and helpful, but not many of us will call these numbers. What I want to tell everyone is... don't walk around the school alone. If you don't have someone to walk with, walk with me if we're going the same way. In fact, I'm inviting you to walk with me or any of the cheerleaders or football players. We don't think that violence is the answer and I'm asking the student council to come up with a plan to stop the bullies in this school. Having gone through this now, I agree it's important to report it to your counselor and if you're too shy to do it alone, ask one of us, and we'll go with you. We can be creative and find better ways to handle bullies. 'Never accept it' is my new slogan and if you want to use it, go ahead, just never accept bullying."

The applause is deafening, and Officer White is smiling at me and nodding his head. He calms the students and adds, "We are here for you, and if you have problems the line starts here. Otherwise, you're dismissed to your last classes and sports.

Now that seems positive, we just have to work on it and continue to implement our plan. Jimmy holds my hand and doesn't even flinch at the sweat that has covered my palm from speaking out. We walk to the Student Council room that I need to be in before sports.

"I'm proud of you, Ness. You did good back there. I'll be at practice when you get out of here, but Caro will be with you, make sure and walk together."

"I will," I answer and squeeze his hand then enter to make sure the dance plans are on schedule and implement the Never Accept Bullying plan.

9

PROBLEM AVERTED

THE WIND IS WHIPPING AROUND WHEN I DROP JIMMY OFF AT Jaden's house and head home. Pulling into the drive, I notice everyone is home. Now that's different. It takes me time to get my car covered, but I finally wrestle the cover into place and walk into the house and am met by my family. They usually aren't in the kitchen, so I'm wondering what's up when Nina glares and says, "What took you so long to get home? We've been waiting for ages. Plans are necessary to protect the twins, and you need to know them."

My dad is serious but rolls his eyes at her tone. "Nina, please."

She huffs and lets him take over with a wave. "We are sorry that you have gone through so much, Vanessa. The twins are not as strong as you, and we believe that it's time we moved them to a school in France. Your mother and I are making plans to get a home there. We need you here to look after our home here. Plus, I don't want a fight with your grandparents if you're too far away for them to see you often enough. You'll be eighteen next month anyway. I trust you to behave and do a good job with the care of our assets here." I can't hide my smile and don't try but, really Jacob, she's not my mom!

Nina sniffs her disapproval and adds, "Don't think we won't be checking the cameras, this is still my house." Point made you're still an anus maw. Asshole isn't big enough for her.

The faces of the twins are beaming, they're bouncing on their toes. This solves my problem. Now, I won't have to ask my grandparents if I can move in. My shoulders relax, and I stiffen my features, not letting the step-demon see my relief. She could, and certainly would use it against me in the future.

My dad takes my hand and says, "I don't think your grandparents would be happy if I took you so far away from them. I will if you want to go through." Nina's eyes widen, then hood in anger.

I say, "No, Jacob, I think your plan is the best, and I'll stay here. You're right about Grandma and Papa Miller. They'll want me close to them until college at least."

Everyone breathes a sigh of relief and relaxes, my dad says, "We are filling out the forms for the academy the girls wish to attend tonight. We will be staying until after the Valentine's party the twins have planned. It would be a big letdown for them not to get their party. They want fireworks, and it can be a going away party for us too."

Yes, Jacob let's make this about you and them. "I'll be happy if you're happy," I say.

"Good, let's go to dinner. I have lots of work to do when we return and need a few minutes first."

Dad drives us to a hotel restaurant on the far side of town, and we have a surprisingly civil family meal. I take a mental picture of everything in the room. I'm practicing knowing my surroundings better.

We are starting dessert when Cilla catches me staring at our waitress she says, "It's rude to stare, but if you like her, you should ask her to the party, Vanessa."

"Oh no, is that how I look? I'm studying people and my surroundings so that I can get good at this and be better at knowing my surroundings. I have a psychology class that I need to write a report for and studying people is part of it. But she is stunning."

Nina raises a brow and grimaces then schools her features into a sucking a sour lemon pose before she says, "Gawking is rude. Keep your eyes on your plate and don't eat all your dessert you don't want to get any curvier dear."

My fork clinks on my plate as I set it down too hard and huff. I know not to eat in front of her, it's always something.

Dad deflects any possible retort by saying, "That was wonderful. Is everyone ready to leave?" Without waiting for an answer, he motions to our waitress for the check. When she lays it on the table in front of Dad, I notice that there is a small tear in the seam of her blouse. My purse is next to me, and I sneak a hand in to find a small roll of duct tape I keep for emergency purposes and palm it.

I leave the table last, and when I pass the girl I smile, reach out my hand and cover her palm transferring the tape to her, and say, "That was very good, tell the chef for me will you?"

She smiles back after a quick peek and says, "I will miss. Have a wonderful evening."

The drive home is a gift of silence. Nina and the twins are glued to their phones. The landscape in this desert land might be different than most cities, but it's beautiful, and I watch it for our short trip back to the house.

When we get home, I go straight to my room, feeling there's no reason to give Nina a chance to start a fight. Besides, I do have school work, and I also want to plan a chart of the information Jimmy wrote about who has what class and who can walk with whom. That gives me an idea. I'm going to make some forms for the student cork board to start a buddy sign up. I know Caro can make us a student program and put it in the student notifications app too if I remember to ask her. I type all the plans and print several forms then text Caro asking what she thinks. She says it'll be easy and will work something up to have ready to implement when the student council votes and it's approved. I text Jimmy laying across my bed with my feet in the air.

. . .

Me: I can't quit thinking about your baby blues. How are you tonight? I have so much to tell you, but it can wait until the morning.

Him: I'm okay and thinking about your butt and long legs.

Me: What?

Him: Oh, hell, Ness. That was Jaden's little brother, he thinks he's being funny. I have got to quit leaving my phone on the bed.

Me: Well, you can think about my butt and legs if you want to. I think about yours a lot. Lol! Just wanted to say goodnight and I'll pick you up in the morning. XOXO

Him: Muah, goodnight gorgeous. Dreaming of your butt now.

WHEN I GET to the kitchen for breakfast the next morning, the cook has a plate ready and sets it on the bar for me. She also hands me a protein bar and a thermal cup full of peppermint mocha coffee. I must be pretty obvious, maybe I should try changing things up some. Nope, not gonna.

I say, "I've been so wrapped up in my own world I've been rude. My name is Vanessa, and my friends call me Ness or Nessa. Thank you for helping me, and I love your food."

"My name is Catherine, my friends call me Kate, Ness. I was thinking that I might be invisible in this house. Thank you for talking to me. I'll make you something special tonight if you want. What do you like?"

"Oh, cool! Kate, I like anything with fruit. There is this grilled chicken salad at the diner that is sooo good. It has pineapple, mandarin oranges, and apples. I'd say cheeseburgers, but my family would really hate that."

"I'll see what I can do and then when your family is gone to France we can make cheeseburgers. Better get going, you don't want to be late picking up that boyfriend of yours."

My eyes widen, "You would be right. Laters, Kate."

10

THE APOLOGY

CRAZY GOOD HAPPINESS FILLS ME THIS MORNING, AND I CAN only hope it stays this way. Jimmy has his hand on my leg as I pull into the parking spot and stop. The feeling is beautiful and makes me happy then I stiffen seeing Terry Counts' terror buddies walking up to my car. I don't open the door, but I roll the window down about half way. My legs start to shake, but I square my shoulders and stare them in their faces, refusing to look scared. In fact, I have on my cheerleader 'bring it on face.'

One of them named Ramon Garza says, "Vanessa, we were wrong to back up Terry, and we're sorry. We can't take it back, so what can we do to make it better?"

He couldn't have surprised me more if he had said he's a baby whale. While I sit gapping, he adds, "I never meant to hurt anyone. Somehow, I just got caught up with the group and just never stood up for what is right. If it's any consolation, fuckin' Terry has been sent to The Spring, a boy's home, for a year for attacking you. He can't hurt you, and we're here to make sure that no one does that again in this school."

"Well, that's a good thing. But, Ramon, actions speak louder than words. The students here have been abused by your crowd for a long time. I think you'll need to prove yourself. I'm not sure we can believe you," I answer through gritted teeth.

Yeah, that hit a nerve. He jerks a bit and blinks then wipes a sneer away and chuffs, "We deserve your shitty words but give us a chance, will ya?"

"I'll tell you what, Ramon. I have several people on my list that have no protection from the likes of you. They need to walk to class without being harassed by bullies. You take my list, find someone who's going your way, watch over them, and keep them company without hurting them, and I'll consider it."

"Give me the fuckin' list, Vanessa, and I'll show you I can be good. All of us can."

"Okay, I'll give it to you at lunch, but if any of your friends take up your slack on the torture end, I'll know. We aren't putting up with this anymore."

He opens my door and makes a gallant hand motion to exit. I look at Jimmy, he nods so I carefully exit my car and stand as far away from our ostensibly rehabilitated bullies as possible.

Jimmy unfolds his tall body and steps out, walking over to me, he puts his arm around my shoulders and grins at the reformed group. No words pass his lips as we saunter by them into the schoolyard and to our lockers.

"Do you think he's for real or maybe it's just a plan to take advantage and fool us before they pull an epic trick on someone?" I ask Jimmy.

"With that group, it could be anything. Make sure the cheerleaders know to watch them with the students. I'll text all the football players with the warning."

We continue walking up the path past the Cave Bear statue that's been there since the first group of students who attended this school bought it with fundraisers. It's a beautiful piece of art. I can't help but be proud of it as our mascot. It's mostly man-shaped but with a bear head and a club in its clawed hands. I smooth a hand over him as we pass as I often do. When we get to our lockers, I open mine with ease. Jimmy kisses me quick and moves to his own locker getting his books for class and a few copies of the list to give out. I have a larger pile of the docs that I stick in my book as we take off for homeroom. Caro meets me with a hug and a smile.

"Hey, I heard that Ramon Garza is going to help with the walking-guard against bullies now? Can I have him, he's adorable?"

"Right, cute like Papa's toenails. Yes, he said he would, but that remains to be seen. And, to be honest, I never noticed his looks. He's always been so mean that I've just thought he's ugly inside and out. Are you crazy, girl? I thought you were all about Joe."

"Are you fucking blind, Ness? No, I get it, all you can see is your quarterback. Yeah, I like Joe a lot but the more, the merrier, right? Don't lie, I see you ogle the Cave Bear all the time." She laughs, and I laugh with her and agree for fun, but Jimmy is all I want... forever.

"Remind me at lunch to give him the list of students who still need someone to walk with, will you Caro?"

"Sure. Do you need me to print some?" She pulls out her phone to open the doc, but I stop her and say, "No, I have several here. I just need to remember to give them out."

Mike a few seats up overheard and asks if he can have a copy, so I hand him one with a smile. This might take off; more and more students are getting on board with the plan.

Caro says, "I added it to the school webpage too, so we can all interact with the comments. Mr. Cobb even commented."

She smiles, and I ask, "Were there many who need someone to walk with?"

"No, almost everyone has a friend to walk with, but some are holding back. Let's make a point of noticing when someone is alone and just walk up as friends to talk and walk along, so they aren't embarrassed."

"You're a genius, Caro. I understand that some of the teachers feel their hands are tied because of getting sued and following school rules. But they want to help, and this will help."

"I accept your praise and only ask one favor... spread the news of my genius," she says in her best fake Latino-British accent. We both giggle and get to work on our school work. Today's class is mostly reading. That makes it pretty hard for us to talk, so instead of risking the wrath of our teacher, we focus on our books.

When the bell for the next class rings, we separate and find our walking buddies. Then, the weirdest thing happens. I don't mean weird like, a tornado in your grandpa's outhouse, I mean weird like a fart in church and everyone begins to sing your praises for finally showing them the light of proper flatulence weird. Ramon, one of my personal tormentors over the last year, walks with me to my next class. He's just part of the group of kids, but it's proof he's trying. I hand him my list, now I won't have to remember to give it to him at lunch. He hums as he looks it over then nods at me.

I say, "Just in case y'all didn't notice, the school webpage has a post made by Caro about the walking-guard, and there are comments from a few who need company. You probably already saw it, but I want to throw it out there just in case you haven't."

As we walk by the Cave Bear, I notice that part of the pedestal he's standing on is splotched with offensive words and hateful remarks. "What the hell? Look at this, will ya? Who would do this, shit?" I'm mad about this. My grandmother's class is who did fundraisers for several years to pay the artist to make our school mascot and the area where he stands. I've always loved the art and can't imagine why people would vandalize it.

"Really, who would do this?" repeats one of the other students with us.

"Great, what is it with this generation? So many have to tear stuff up just to get attention. I'll add another post to the school site later about vandals. We need to add that as an action in the council meeting too, Ness," says Caro.

"Yeah, that'll be as welcome as being stuck in your grandpa's outhouse in July. But... you do have a point. There's a lot of vandalized stuff around the school these days. Maybe we could have a student work day. I can bring sodas and make cupcakes or something for help. What do you think, Caro, maybe some others will bring stuff to get people here to help?"

"I think it's a great idea. What are you doing after school, anyway?" Caro answers.

"I'm not sure. Should we ask the others if they want to meet at the diner and get a burger before we go home?"

"Good idea, I'll tell you at practice who can come," she says.

We split off and go into our quads for class. Mine is math, and for some reason, I can't math today. It's like my brain wants to, but it keeps burping instead. Instead, I write notes for the council meeting... including all the topics I'd like to bring up.

11

DOWN BOY

THE CAFETERIA IS STUFFED WITH TEENS TODAY. ALL THE students who usually wander around campus or eat outside are even in here. Maybe... Mr. Winn will let me announce the walking-guards being on the school website. Everyone could be in here because there's safety in numbers.

They have enchiladas on the menu too, and our cafeteria ladies can cook. This is one day I'll eat more than just my fruit. The school's enchiladas are the best food on the planet. No one disagrees. I thank Mrs. Brown, one of our gourmet enchilada chefs, when going through the line and paying. When I get to our regular table, I set my tray down beside Jimmy, who is talking with Joe and Caro.

"Hey, beautiful, how's your day?" Jimmy asks.

"Well, I think we've made progress in the bullying area, but I have another problem?"

"Oh hell, did someone else try something? Tell me who and I'll just kick their ass," he says with a grin. Jimmy's way too smart to go beat someone up. Now if he caught them in the middle of hurting me, it would get tactical rapidly.

"No, I've noticed some vandalism around the school. There's an increase in this type of vandalism, especially around the Cave Bear."

"What? I guess we can ask around to see if anyone saw who is doing it. I heard you want to have burgers after school. So... can I have the rest of your enchiladas?"

"No way, but you can have my cake," I tease, pulling my tray closer to me and smiling at my boy.

Caro laughs at me and makes room for Zane by scooting her chair closer to Joe's. She says, "Don't look at me. I'm not even going to share my cake."

"You guys are no fun. I guess I'll just have to go get Mrs. Brown to give me some seconds." My boy jumps up and takes off toward the line, the rest of us continue to talk.

Joe is excited about an idea and says, "You guys know my dad works for an oil company and they have lots of new hires in this area. I've noticed, working in the office, we have new kids enrolling and wonder if they'll need help getting around school. What if we talk to Principal Smart and ask if they can have mentors for their first week? We did that in my old school in Alabama, and it really helped me. We could let them know, right up front, how we're not putting up with bullies and what they should do if that happens."

The Cueva Hallow High School system has mentor programs for seniors to get them ready for the real world and work in their chosen fields. Joe wants to work in the schools as administrative help and work his way up in the district as the head administrator of schools in the county. He has some great ideas to help young people get a good education.

Everyone loves the idea and tells him so. That's a great idea, Joe. How many new students do we have starting? Do you know?" I ask.

"There are four this week. They're already signed up and suppose to have their first day tomorrow," says Joe.

"Well, I'll go to the office after lunch and get on it. Who wants to be an escort for a week? I need to have volunteers when I ask," he responds.

I ask, "How many girls and how many boys Joe? I think we should use boys for the girls and girls for the boys. What do y'all think?"

"Good idea, there are three boys and one girl," he answers with wide excited eyes.

"I would have loved a pretty cheerleader to walk with me when I started here," says Jimmy as he sits back down beside me with his second helping of enchilada gold.

"You nut, you lived here and had a tour with us all when we were in Jr. High." I laugh and punch him lightly on the shoulder.

"So, you're saying you noticed me before now?" He winks and smiles, sheepishly.

"No, not really... of course, I did! You just never gave me the time of day before," I tease.

"Okay, you two. It's getting deep. Nessa, let's make like Moses and get the flock out of here," Caro says, standing and jerks her head for me to follow.

"We're going to the office. I'll see you in a bit," I say winking at my blue-eyed jock. I give him a quick peck on the cheek and the table 'Ahs' at us, and my face turns red. Yeah, but I'd do it again.

When I turn, Travis Parks sticks out a foot and trips me. I fall forward and hit my elbow on the floor, my phone sliding halfway across the cafeteria. Zane who had just walked into the room rushes to pick it up for me and comes over to help. An irate Jimmy is already helping me up. When he's sure I'm okay he turns to face Travis and yanks him up by his shirt collar his fists tighten as he yells, "You little piece of shit. I'm gonna beat you like the punk-ass bitch you..." Not waiting, Zane and Joe hold him back to keep him from hitting the dirtbag.

"She deserves it and more. She almost got me suspended for nothing this morning. I had to beg to stay in school, and I'm in free studies for a month until I prove I can get along with people. All because of her!" Travis shouts in Jimmy's face then spits on his shirt. That did it! New values against violence or not that's the last straw, and his struggle for freedom intensifies as Zane and Joe battle to restrain him.

Mr. Winn, the cafeteria monitor, steps up in Travis' face. Standing in between him and Jimmy, he says, "Mr. Parks come with me. You have a lot of explaining to do. Mr. Danforth, you need to calm down and escort Miss Cutter to the nurse's office. Miss Cutter after you've seen the nurse, please meet us in Principal Smart's office."

While we all start to do exactly as Mr. Winn told us, Jimmy jerks away from his friends and offers me his hand. "Babe, let me go with you to the nurse."

I shake my head up and down, tears begin to flood my eyes. Jimmy put his arm around me. Our whole group bunches together and moves off with us. I see them shake their heads as we leave, angry at Travis, but worry fills their eyes for me. The 'lunch is over' bell rings, and our friends split off for class.

"I'm going unless you need me, chica. Let me know what happens. I'll see you later," Caro says and hugs me before leaving. I bob my head that I will and let her go.

I think I really messed up my arm. It is aching, and I can't turn my wrist without it sending a sharp pain all the way to my hand. More tears leak out of my eyes now that we're away from the others. Jimmy hugs me being careful of the arm I'm holding. I look up and ask, "Were you really going to punch Travis?"

"No, I was going to beat him within an inch of his life."

I can't hold back a stupid sound as I say, "Don't ever do that. Please! I don't want you hurt."

"I wouldn't get hurt, but he would've."

"Well then make me a deal. Promise me you'll never fight at school. You need to stay in school and get your diploma. I have plans for us, and my parents will never let me see you if you get kicked out of school. I don't want you to fight at all. It'll only get you into trouble with the law. Find another way maybe... a taser?" I grin.

He can't help it and laughs at my suggestion. "Okay, Ness, I promise. You're right, maybe a taser straight to his nut sack would be a good idea."

When we reach the nurse's office, and I pick up the pencil to sign myself in. I fail. I can't write because it hurts too much. Jimmy spots Mrs. Sanders and says, "I'm going to sign in Vanessa. She can't write because she fell and hurt her arm."

The nurse says, "That's all right, sign her in and stay here." She points to a chair beside her desk then adds, "I'm taking her back to look at her and let her rest."

Jimmy nods to her, winks at me, then fills in the form to sign me into the nurse's office.

In a separate room, Nurse Saunders has me sit then looks at my arm and says, "Vanessa, can you move your arm at all?"

"Yes, ma'am, I can I just can't use my hand without it hurting, and I can't turn it over without pain. I'm sure something's messed up."

"Well, I think you need an X-ray and a visit to your doctor. I'm going to call your parents to come to pick you up. You can rest on the cot or just stay sitting in the chair. I'll be right back."

12

IT'S BROKEN

After Mrs. Sanders called my dad, his secretary, Jane Perry, shows up to check me out of school and take me to the hospital for the x-rays. Her pressed office wear looks perfect on her slight body and not a hair is out of place on her brunette bun. She raises her glasses a little on our way out the door of the nurse's office when Jimmy holds the door, so I don't have to use my arm.

Jane dismisses him by saying, "Thank you, young man, you can leave now. We appreciate your help."

I shake my head as the smile leaves my face and say, "Jane, this is Jimmy Danforth. He's the Cave Bear quarterback and my boyfriend. He brought me to the nurse's office. "Jimmy, I'll text you from the hospital. Go to class and please let Caro and Tween know I'm going to miss practice and will text them tonight. If you don't mind, please?"

I shocked Jane. The look on her face turns stony, and she moves us away at a fast clip. As we get to her car, and she clicks her key fob to unlock it and says, "Vanessa, does your father know about Jimmy Danforth?"

Uh oh, she knows his last name. "No, he doesn't know much. He doesn't really have much to do with me. I tried to tell him once, though."

"I suggest you keep that boy a secret or all hell will break loose. There's no telling what your mother would do if she found out you're dating the Killer of Cueva Hallows son."

I start to defend him, but she stops me and says, "I don't blame him he was a victim... and girl... he is fine!" She giggles, and now I'm the one who is surprised. I can't remember her ever being normal just a rigid rule keeper who does Jacob's every wish. Which is taking care of what I need, in most cases.

"She isn't my mother, but he is really cute, isn't he? Please, don't tell Jacob. I know it won't go well."

"I'll keep your secret and if it comes out that I knew I'll lie, so keep it to yourself. You want to stop for a drink on the way to the hospital?"

"Oh, yes, I'm parched."

Jane drives to the Sonic drive-through and gets us a soda. Then we go to the hospital and wait forever in the waiting room. I text Jimmy, Caro, Tween, Cess, and Cilla, so they know that I'm still waiting and don't know anything yet. Gossip travels like wildfire in our little town if I don't keep someone in the loop the story could become a horror story.

Staring at my phone and waiting for a response, I hear, "Miss Cutter, Vanessa Cutter?"

I nod to the nurse and get up to go toward her. Jane gets up and goes in with me.

After the general triage questions, the nurse leads us to a separate room and sits me on a patient examination table. She asks if she can see my arm and says, "Can you extend your arm for me." I do, and she hands me a bottle of water and continues, "Now turn your hand over for me please."

"Ouch, that really hurts! I can do it, but it hurts... a lot."

"Oh, I know, I'm sorry." She takes the bottle from me, and

another nurse enters the room. She tells him that I have a possible broken elbow and to please escort me to X-ray.

The X-ray technician has to position and reposition, bend and straighten my elbow. After the second time she had to move it, I begin to cry. It's getting harder to move, and I can't help myself. When I get back to my exam room, Jane is talking to my dad on her cell.

"She is just now getting X-rays, I'll call again when we know something. Yes, bye." She looks up at me and sees that I've been crying. Blinking, she asks, "Did they hurt you, Vanessa?"

"Yes, but not on purpose, they had to position my arm and it hurt. I can't move it very easy anymore. It hurts more than a big dog... and a small one too." I deadpan.

She smiles and says, "Do you want me to ask for something for the pain?"

"Yes, if they'll give me something. I could use it."

Doctor Vargas is my doctor and has been since I was born. He's a serious man on the shorter side of average with dark hair shot with silver. He walks into the room and says, "Well Vanessa, you've broken your elbow. It's a classic break. Even with the swelling, it can be seen easily on the X-rays. If it were any bigger, you would need surgery. As it is, I want you in a sling for two weeks. Don't use it much. I won't be putting it in a cast either. That will only limit your use in the future and make it heal stiffer than if we leave one off. You can have something for pain for a few days if you like. Do you want Ibuprofen 600 or Tylenol 3?"

"I think the Ibuprofen works better on me, Doc. Do you mind if I have some now?"

"That will be fine." He nods in the direction of the nurse, and she hurries off to get me some. He writes on my chart and says, "I'll see you in my office in two weeks for another X-ray, and then we'll start you on therapy."

"Yes sir, will you write me an excuse for sports class? I'm a cheer-leader and need to be excused from participating."

He nods, and after scribbling out the excuse, he says, "Here you go, young lady. I know you're an active girl, but I want you to rest that arm. I'll send the nurse back in with your sling. Do you have questions?"

"No, sir, I've got it. No using it for two weeks, follow up, then therapy."

He smiles at me, pats me on my good shoulder, and leaves the room.

"Well, Nina isn't going to like this at all. What do you want to bet she says I did this on purpose for attention and how much it costs her?"

Jane responds, "I wish it were easier on you, but they'll be out of all our hair in just a few days. After the twin's party, we'll have some breathing room. She's hard on everyone but her girls. I, for one, won't be sad to see her go." She stops herself with a look like she said too much.

I smile and touch her hand and say, "You and me both!"

The nurse comes in just then and asks, "Okay Vanessa, we're a little short on slings, but I have Cave Bear blue, white, or rainbow. Which one do you want?"

The white one will get dirty fast. The rainbow one looks like the My Little Ponies exploded all over it. The blue one is the one, so I answer, "Blue, please."

She puts the sling on me and repeats Dr. Vargas' instructions then hands Jane a stack of paperwork, saying, "You ladies are free to go."

When we get to the car, Jane tucks the papers into my school bag and says, "I hope you don't mind that all these years I'm the one who has taken you to your appointments and shown up for emergencies? I know your father loves you. I'm sure he isn't sure what to do where you're concerned, primarily because he feels he has to make Nina happy."

"No, I don't mind. I feel like you're more family to me than them. We're friends, right?"

"Yes, very much so. Especially since Nina has demanded that

while they are gone, I must keep an eye on you." She laughs and makes the motion of pointing two fingers at her eyes then at me.

"I'm duly warned, I laugh back and add, "Now do you mind leaving me at the diner? My friends were going to meet there after school, and I want to see if they're still there."

She leaves me at the diner where I see Caro, Joe, Jimmy, and Tween. I walk in sporting my new sling and move to the table where they're sitting. Jimmy spots me. First, his worried face makes me feel bad, so I smile. He smiles, but it's a fraction of his usual brilliant grin. He rushes over, tenderly puts his arm around me, and seats me in his chair. He slides another one over from the neighboring table and sits beside me.

Everyone speaks at once. It turns out that Travis is in as much trouble as Terry and has been expelled. Mr. Brown witnessed the entire incident and didn't hold back telling Principal Smart.

Caro says, "And everyone is wondering if your dad is going to sue the Parks for damages."

I say, "I doubt it. Nina is going to have him so busy with the twin's party this weekend and moving that he won't have time to think about me. That reminds me, are all of you coming to the party?"

Everyone but Jimmy says they wouldn't miss it. Jimmy says, "I wanted to talk to you about that."

Tween says, "This is going to get serious... I'm going. You want to come with me, Caro?"

"Yes, yes, I do," Caro replies.

Joe says, "I'm out of here too."

Jimmy puts a hand out to his friend and says, "Can you wait for me outside we need a ride back to Nessa's car."

"Sure, I'll wait outside in my car."

Jimmy is searching the ground and says, "Nessa, if I go to the party, it'll cause all sorts of problems. What if I just meet you under the train bridge? We can dance there. It's so close we could probably hear the music just as well from your backyard."

I'm instantly let down then think for a minute and say, "You're right, and we'll be able to do a lot more at the Valentine's dance before the party anyway. Let's go to the dance then I'll go home and meet you under the bridge at nine. If I can't sneak out, I'll text."

His smile is killer, and he hugs me to his muscular body. I squeak a little scream, and he backs off, his face red with embarrassment and apologizes for hurting my arm. We get up to pay his bill and meet Joe in the parking lot for our ride.

13

THE DANCE PLANS

WHEN I GET HOME, I TELL MY FAMILY DR. VARGAS'S instructions and give Dad my paperwork from the hospital. No one really pays any attention. Even Jacob but he does say he's sorry my elbow is broken as he takes the paperwork. He does this, while not looking at me then proceeds to tap out more work on his computer totally forgetting I'm standing there.

I don't care that Nina doesn't care. Anyway, she's wrapped up in planning the twin's after party for Valentine's... which includes a fireworks show. I know my sisters are spoiled, it isn't their fault. In any case, I get to tag along on this, to a degree... sort of.

Valentine's is today, but since it's Thursday, we'll celebrate and have the dance tomorrow on Friday. We certainly can't have a party that might not be the best, most attended party for Nina's precious little twinsies.

Dealing with my family is such an effort in protecting myself from being let down or hurt that I stay away as much as possible. Even if Nina isn't yelling at or threatening me. Them pretending I don't exist is sometimes worse than the yelling. At least when I'm being yelled at, they have to acknowledge my existence.

I come home after being taken to the ER for being attacked at school... I have a broken elbow... nobody came to check on me at the hospital... to be ignored, again... yep sounds like the world is working for them. A thing I learned a long time ago, I can't let the way they treat me change my outlook on the planet, or my friends and class-mates. I'll soldier on and ultimately succeed. Not feeling too poorly, I go to the kitchen and pour myself a bowl of cereal for dinner and go to bed. Problems encountered, sure... problems solved... all that could be. Yep, I rock! A private smile breaks out on my face as I go to my room.

THIS MORNING MY ARM HURTS! To make matters worse, I can't seem to accomplish my usual morning routine. Well, sure I can shower, brush my teeth... stuff like that. It only takes one arm. The problems come when I need two hands. Which, by the way, is way more often than I imagined. I need two hands for a ponytail. To be honest, I never thought about that, but I'm thinking about it now. If last night taught me anything, it taught me to take care of my own problems. I can't put my hair in a ponytail, heck I'll leave it down.

Next problem is my shirt. Nope, I'll slip my bad arm into the tee sleeve, slide the rest over my head and pop my other arm through. Jeans... well, I can't button them, so a skirt with an elastic waistband will fix that problem. Tennis shoes, a big nope. I'll simply stuff my feet into a pair of slides. Victory! Clothes—zero, Vanessa—let's see, hair, tee shirt, jeans, shoes count as two. So, Vanessa — five!

Happy after my clothing victory, I take off for the kitchen with some Ibuprofen in hand. Kate meets me with coffee and one of the fattest breakfast burritos I can remember.

She says, "You didn't eat much last night, so here, this is better than cereal. I made one for your boyfriend too." She points to an even more massive burrito wrapped in foil sitting on the granite bar.

"Thank you, Kate. I gotta go though it took me too long to get ready this morning, and I refuse to be late." I stuff my breakfast into my book bag, toss it over my good shoulder, grab my coffee, and give Kate a brilliant smile and wave as I leave.

Today's the day the new students are assigned to the volunteer guides, so it isn't surprising when I'm called to the office via the intercom along with Caro, Joe, and Supe. My student is gorgeous. His name is Josh Turner, tall, dark, and handsome. Maybe, I should trade with Caro. I look over and see that her guy is just as cute, all the new students are extremely attractive.

Mrs. Smart introduces us and says, "For you, new students, you will be with your tour guides and fellow students for the next week. However, if at the end of that week, you think you aren't familiar enough we can extend your affiliation for one additional week. Your guides will help you find each of your classes. They will also assist you with any other issues pertaining to school for the week. I want you, members of the student council, to show them to their classes and cafeteria and explain things as you go like where to obtain PE clothes and such. Do you have any questions?"

We all chorus, "No, ma'am."

Excited that our plan is in progress, we leave with the new enrollees and show them to class.

Josh, the student assigned to me, says, "When the principal introduced us, she told you my name is Josh, but my friends call me Joker. You can call me Joker, too if you want." He's a little shy when he says this and is staring at his feet before he looks up at me to check my reaction.

That's a different kind of nickname. I wonder what he did to get it and say, "I have a nickname too, Joker. You can call me Ness or Nessa if you like. Did they tell you there's a dance tomorrow night?"

"They did, would you like to go with me, Ness?"

"Well, Joker, I have a boyfriend and am going with him. But maybe we can dance together."

"That'll be my pleasure." He smiles.

When I walk into homeroom, Jimmy is waiting for me. I introduce Joker, and they hit it right off. I breathe a sigh of relief at no show of jealousy.

As the day goes on, I can't wait for it to be over. My arm hurts, and I just want to go to sleep. Jimmy meets me in the parking lot after school. I leave Joker now that he's at his truck and walk toward my boyfriend.

My handsome boy says, "Ness, I can tell you don't feel good. Do you want me to drive you home?"

"No, that would just cause a shit storm. I can do it. I'll text you later though. Do you have something to match me for the dance tomorrow? I'm wearing black with a little turquoise heart intertwined in a pink one."

"Yep, remember my teal polo? I washed it as soon as you told me on our first date."

"Okay, I'm not thinking, I'll see you in the morning."

THE NEXT DAY the whole school is buzzing with excitement, and absolutely none of us are paying attention to our studies. The teachers get it, and an announcement is made after lunch that because of the dance we'll be dismissed at 2:00 p.m. today. The twins call Nina and tell her, so she makes them a hair appointment and says she'll meet them there. I'm left out but ask, "You think she would let me go Cess?"

"I don't care what she thinks you're coming with me. They take walk-ins all the time, and we could all get mani-pedis!"

She's so excited I decide to brave anything Nina might do. It's a nice time anyway because Nina ignores me. I keep quiet. No reason to give her a reason to be upset. Cilla gets the cutest nails with little crystal bears and red hearts on black lacquer. Cess picks white with different colored hearts on each finger and toe. I get pink with turquoise crystal hearts on my pointer fingers and big toes. When we leave, I go straight home, and Nina takes the twins to get new shoes.

Going to the back door, I overhear Jacob on the phone. He's talking business, so after catching just a little, I stop listening. I don't care what color he needs something like art to be, but it sounds like his company might be struggling some. Nope, I'm not interested. I go to my room to dress then text Jimmy that I'll meet him at the dance. He sends me a picture of him with a big smile and says he is ready and waiting.

14

THE CAVE BEAR

Halstein

THE ORANGE, DUSKY SUNSET IS STILL PEAKING ABOVE THE western hills behind Cueva Hallow High School as all the teachers and staff file out of the buildings. Yet they'll return soon enough to chaperone the annual Valentine's Day dance tonight. I'm here, like every year since I've made this a place to watch and protect. My name is Halstein, my family calls me Hal. I'm known as the Cave Bear by humans who don't know I'm alive. I'm a gargoyle and will enjoy the party from my perch on the roof of the main building.

I watch from there to help the humans when I can. One of my missions is to watch for evil, which can hurt my people, the Ceorfan Guild. I've stood guard at this post for several decades. It was my pleasure to watch over our Queen, Kendra Macbard, when she first came to this high school. It was my honor to act as her protector during those years, and I was equally honored to protect her brothers,

Jared and Dana. I've officially met them since they've been integrated into the Guild. They're every bit as worthy of their station as any of our past Queens or Princes.

During the day I watch for... What is this? Two young men are coming toward me carrying something. I know these two. They have visited me before.

"Hurry Terry, I don't think we should be here and I sure as hell don't want to get caught damaging school property," says Dalton, one of Terry's thug acolytes who blindly follow his every command.

"Fucker, just do what I tell you. Hand me the sledge if you ain't too chicken shit. If you are, fuck off, and I'll do it myself," smears Terry.

"Terry," Dalton starts, "I thought you had to stay with your parents since you were turned over to them by the court. How did you take off without them seeing you leave, anyway?"

"They never notice whether I'm there or not. They don't care. Anyway, this ain't the time for twenty questions. I'm here to fuck up the Cave Bear before the dance. I want it to look like shit for that stupid fucking party. I want those assholes to know not to mess with my stuff while I'm gone. I also want everyone in my crew to know. Tomorrow, you tell them what I did tonight. Tell them I'll do the same to them if they don't do what I say, even if I'm not here." Terry swings the sledgehammer and nails the Cave Bear to punctuate his words.

Ohhh, hell that hurts! That little shit just hit my hand with what looks like a five-pound sledgehammer. He broke off a couple of fingers if I'm right. He's swinging again. Holy cow! Big chips fly off of my leg, hell that hurts! Even as stone, I have the sense of feel.

Sunset is on us now, and I feel the change come over me. Torping is what we call the process a gargoyle goes through when we change to stone in the daylight hours. It heals everything on our bodies, and when we wake or untorp at sundown, we are healed and whole. As my body changes, I feel the magic crackling and a sound like shattered glass. I'm not going to do too much, but these little shits deserve a scare. I haven't been caught moving by a human in decades. They usually pass it off like it's nothing and pretend it didn't happen. I don't roar or stretch, I just turn my large hairy head and gape at them... one pisses himself while the other runs without looking back. The frozen pee whiz finally gets his brain wound up and joins the other on a dead run.

"Hey, what are you boys doing over there?" I hear a voice that I recognize as Principal Smart's. I watch as those little assholes keep running. She can't see who they are, because they're too far away. She doesn't even look at me, so I stand stiff and unmoving.

Shit! No, leave them alone... I watch as she looks down at the chips of stone that shithead broke from my torped body. She picks up my broken fingers from the ground. I don't like it when a piece of me is broken off, and someone takes it. It's never been a problem when they notice I've been 'repaired' the next time they see me as stone. But I don't like taking chances either. Oh well, can't fix it now. I'm sure it'll give Principal Smart something to ponder on at some point.

I hear her mumble, "Can't have anything nice around these kids anymore." I watch her as she hurries away, shaking her head still gripping. I don't even try to hear her. I've listened to pretty much everything since I began my watch here, besides it's time for me to leave.

I have to go home to Navan, the last gargoyle city. I need to report in, and I want to ask our Royal Mage, Jericho, for some magic help. I want to talk to him about a new spell stone to help with the bullies at this school. Maybe the old mage has one that will temper the emotions of these kids, and I won't have to save any more little girls like I did earlier.

Jericho gave me a stone a long time ago that looks like a caveman's club. I always have it with me, it's on my shoulder when I'm torped, it makes for a striking pose, and yeah, it's always with me when I'm not. The magic of my club allows me to move freely in the daylight hours to help the students if they need help. I haven't needed it in a long time, but the bullies are taking their cruelty to a new level here lately. Attacking that girl, Vanessa, was the last straw.

I'm Ceorfan, and every member of our race has a magical gift. Mine is sonic speed. So when I saw that boy accost Vanessa, I used the magic of the stone club to move. I moved fast. The same way I'm about to move quickly to get my fake statue-self set up, so no one notices a missing statue. I do this every night and usually roam the school grounds or go to my home for meals. We have the best food in the lunchroom in Navan. It only takes me minutes to get there.

I take my job of protecting the teens here seriously, and I'll be back early tonight for the dance. Parties breed trouble, and I need to be here.

I speed to the closet that holds my effigy or ef, my statue, a tall, muscular guy with a bear head, handsome if I do say so myself. I squeeze my large body into the broom closet that only I have the key to.

"Ouch, that hurts," I groan to myself as I scrape the same hand that has just been healed in my change on a sharp shelf sticking out more than I remembered. I quickly grab my ef and lift the fake me onto the pedestal, and like a shot, I'm off to the gargoyle city.

"Jericho, I need the stone soon. I need to get back to the school before their party," I warn.

"I understand, Hal. I know it's here, just give me time. I'll find it," Jericho answers in a monotone voice. He thinks it's funny to talk to me like the computer named HAL in the movie, 2001 *A Space Odyssey*. Unfortunately, it's a little funny.

I continue to watch, helpless, and to be honest a bit frustrated at not being able to speed the old mage up. "Jericho..."

"Oh... here we go." He grins at me, his eyes alight with the fire of a much younger man. He hands me a beautiful crystal blue stone which he's cradling like a baby. Is this going to break when I take it? "This will help control bad tempers at the school?" I ask.

"It will do that and more. All the fighting should be curtailed, and the people in the area will be kinder to each other... most of the time anyway. Is that all I can do for you before you leave?"

"Yes, friend, I'm sorry at my impatience, not any failing on your part."

"You are most welcome, Hal. I understand."

"Thank you again. I need to report to Mega, my Commander, before I leave. So, I hate to demand a spell stone and run. I'll make it up to you on the weekend if you're home." I tip my hand off of my forehead and am out the door before the wizard has a chance to answer.

MY REPORT to Mega describes the vandalism and some of the bullying that has picked up in recent years. "Commander, the bullying is worse this year than it was last year. If you remember, that was one of the worst years since I've been at the school."

"We have been keeping track of your reports, Hal."

Was my Commander now using the HAL 9000 voice?

"Jericho and Kino believe much of it is a result of the rise of Baratium," He finishes.

"Sir, if that's the case, as one of his Elite Warriors, should my duty station be changed to one where I can be part of the force to capture our enemy?" I ask. The Ceorfan race has a military force in which I'm a soldier, and no soldier wants to be left off the battlefield when their friends are in danger.

"No, Hal, you are where you need to be right now. When the time comes, you will be called. For now, protect the children in that school. Now please, I have much to do and will add your report to the information to present to the High Guild and our Queen. Thank you, Hal."

I'm dismissed after my short visit with my boss, so I'm off. Minutes later, I step onto the roof as I return to the school. Tonight, I'll perch here and watch the teens, but first I need to put the crystal stone in my efs hand. That's when I notice how awful the graffiti on the pedestal is, so I take a few minutes and clean it off. I have a rep to uphold.

15

IT'S HERE

I came back to the school early to make sure everything is in place and help with setting the food out for the dance. I stand in the archway to the patio where the dance will be held and take in the scene. Shoulders tight I take a deep breath, recognizing that although it's coming along, it's not finished. I have work to do. I better get at it, so I dive in.

We have most of the decorations up already. All the main building quads face the patio, where the dance will be, making a U shape around the area. No one is going to notice the classroom doors though because the stair rails and guards are covered with lights. It'll be gorgeous when they're turned on. Everything else will be dark except for a little lighting around the food and the fountain. The fountain is a small pool about ten by fourteen feet at the most significant part then narrows two feet wide and travels the entire patio area of the main building the way you might see in an expensive hotel. It's off to one side of the courtyard. The largest part is close to the principal's office in the short section of the U.

It is a hazing rite of passage for freshmen to be shoved into the fountain. It just takes a little bump. They usually get their feet wet, but I have seen people trip and get wetter. A kid will be sloshing with wet feet for the rest of the day. The teachers must hate it, that's probably why the fountain is only running in the summer months. The Cave Bear statue is on a platform at the other end of the patio and is also lit. The decorating council and I surround the base of the platform with blue and white flower arrangements. While we're arranging, I observe that someone has fixed the pedestal. No paint anywhere. How did they do that? When did they do that? The Cave Bear is also holding a stunning, uncut blue crystal. That's beautiful! I wonder where it came from.

When I turn around, Tween is beside me and pulls me in for a big hug. Drawing back, she says, "You look so gorgeous! Come help. The cafeteria ladies made cookies, brownies, some pinwheels, and dip trays. The committee has set them out already but the stuff the council members are bringing needs to be set somewhere. What do you think? Should we add a table?"

"Yeah, we're going to have to," I agree.

Jimmy is walking in, centered between the new boy Joker and Joe. He grins his panty melting grin and rakes my body from head to toe. I shiver with delight before I wave them over and ask, "Do you guys mind getting another table out of the storage room and setting it up over here for extra food?"

"Of course, beautiful, just show me where to get it," Jimmy says motioning to the two boys. They do a half jerk upwards with their heads in acceptance as they move off with their friend when I point to the storage room door.

Caro and Supe are bringing in the punch now and making a punch fountain. It's beautiful when they're finished. A high flowing fall of sherbet goodness that makes the drink table look lovely. They have the help of several other students and have plastic champagne flutes surrounding the fountain on a stark white table cloth. Yeah, that'll stay clean.

Everything in the room is glittery and shines silver, white, and cave bear blue. It is getting close to time, Principal Smart has the custodians turn off the overhead lights from the U's wings, and the area is a fairyland of colors as the strings of twinkling lights give a romantic glow to the area.

While I'm looking around in wonder, warm hands touch my waist softly and stay there. I turn enough to take in my handsome boyfriend looking so good I could eat him.

"Ness, you and the student council have made our school look amazing." The gleam in his eyes is a spark to my needs.

I take a deep breath and sigh leaning back onto his chest, feeling special and say, "Thank you. It took everyone, and you'd be surprised at how good Mrs. Smart is at design and decor. I can't wait for it to start and dance with you."

"We could dance here right now. I don't mind if the band is tuning or playing as long as my arms are around you."

My mouth dries up, and I can't think.

Caro blurts out, "Hey, you two quit cuddling and help with the chips." I pull myself away from Mr. Cuddles, it's time for the band to start. Students are arriving and lining up for their Valentine pictures. We have the photojournalism students and yearbook photographers taking turns for an hour apiece, so they get to have fun at the party also.

I giggle. "You mean, where did we put them, and you want some. I'm going to start calling you the chip monster."

She chuckles, and I pull a box of chips out from under the table and add several packages to a basket. I dump a giant bag of tortilla chips onto the tray next to the guacamole dip too. There, chip crisis averted.

I ask Tween and Caro, "Hey, help restock this as needed and let's pass the word to the other cheerleaders. No need to take a chance on letting the chips empty if I get caught up in Jimmy's baby blues."

"Girl, if you don't, I will! That boy is fine!" Caro hits me on the shoulder lightly and cocks her head shaking it to the music that is starting.

"I promise I will, and I'm not sharing."

Caro slinked up earlier in a sexy little outfit that was even tighter than mine. Instead of a skirt and fancy ripped tee like mine, she has a form fitted short dress showing every curve. I ironed a little pink heart on my sling to match my outfit. She did it right, it isn't low cut or too short but shows all the right stuff. For our clothes to be date style and not formal, we did dress nice.

Almost all of the cheer squad is around us now, so we share where the chips are and tell them it's our job to keep them loaded up. Everyone agrees. "Also," I start, "Mingle and dance... if you see someone holding back go get them to dance or get some food. Maybe have them do a karaoke song later during the band's break. And ladies and gents get to the photo booth and make sure to get your picture taken. Those will be featured in the yearbook. Now disperse and have a blast!"

So, it starts. Jimmy and I wander around and say a quick 'Hi' to all of the students even those who we just know names but never really talk to. After roaming around the patio for a while Jimmy says, "Damn Ness, this is boring. I hope your sisters' party is better than this. No one is dancing. Would you dance with me, maybe if we start some of the others will too?"

I lift my shoulders and reach out a hand to Jimmy and say, "You better believe it, kind sir." Just when he pulls me to him, taking care not to jar my hurt arm a fast song starts. Well, thems the breaks. We separate and speed up our bodies flowing to the music. We're looking pretty good and talk as much as we can past the loud music. Jimmy jerks his head in a 'get out of here' motion. When I glance to see who he is motioning to I watch as Joker and Tween hit the floor with us. On her way, she grabs Caro who drags Joe like a toy behind her. Okay, this is better, and the band starts another song. It's the "Cupid Shuffle" so we all lineup and wave our friends onto the dance floor with us. Everyone can do this. We all know it.

We turn and hoot in laughter when we mess up, and when it's finally over, I'm worn out and holding my arm. That was a workout. I drag Jimmy to a little table away from the crowd. At least many of the other students are dancing now. My cute quarterback says he'll be back after seating me. He gets me some water and him some punch. He got us a whole plate of goodies to share. We dig in and watch our friends dance while we eat.

The line at the photo booth has finally slimmed down, so I ask, "Are you ready to get our pics?"

"Yes, let's get that out of the way and go dance some more."

He guides me over to the backdrop of a cave scene. While posing in front of it, he asks, "I like this one. What do you think?"

"I like it." Although I was talking about him and not the cave scene. It's cool, but my Jimmy is fine! Just as I finish answering, Wally Cline saunters over with a big grin and motions to us, indicating where we should stand.

Wally says, "The first pic is free, then ten dollars if you want a printed one and one set sent to your phone. Jimmy nods and takes out his wallet and gives him the money. Wally gets set, and we pose. He shows us our picture, and it looks funny, so I ask him to redo it while I adjust and try to keep my eyes open this time. He shows us again, and it looks great.

"That looks wonderful Wally, send this one to my phone, please," I ask, but I can't quit looking at the pic. We make a beautiful couple. What is this gorgeous guy doing with me?

The thought no sooner hits my brain when I hear him say, "Holy fuck, baby. I know you're beautiful, but shit, you're too good for me. What did I ever do to deserve you?"

I tilt my head down some and look through my lashes at him and chuff lightly. My chest rises quickly. He makes me feel on top of the world. I respond, "That is what I was thinking about you. Can we go get some real food now? I need to get to my sisters' party or pay the step-monster piper."

"We're out of here. Let's go tell the others we'll see them at the party... well, at least you will. I'll wait for you at the train bridge. We'll still be able to hear the music, and I'll bring a blanket, and we can lay down and watch the stars. What do you think?"

"I think I want Jacob to meet you, but you're probably right. I don't want to ruin the girls' party."

After hugs and promises to see them later, Jimmy and I leave the dance and go to the diner and grab a cheeseburger before we go to my house. The trick will be sneaking out. Naw, they never notice whether I'm there or not.

16

THE FIREWORKS

IT'S GETTING COOL. I'M GOING TO NEED A JACKET TONIGHT. I hope Jimmy has his with him. Now, to get my butt in the house and make an appearance. Maybe, if Nina and Jacob see me, they won't notice when I leave.

I'm standing in the kitchen when a harried and overexcited Nina blows in. She demands that I refill the foods on the buffet that she's set up in the dining area off to the side of the patio. It isn't cold here with so many people. I note that this party is nicer than the school dance. Many of the students that were at the dance are already here and dancing. The twins come over, and even Cilla gives me a big sister hug smiling ear to ear. It warms my heart. I know she loves me even if I'm closer to Cecily. She is closer to Nina and that conflicts with our relationship.

I say, "I'm so happy for you two! Your party rocks! And I have to say it's better than the school dance."

Cilla asks, "You think so? I definitely do. I gotta go and dance with as many people as I can to remember this night. See you later, sis."

What? Wait! Did Cilla just call me *sis*? Cecily and I stare into each other's eyes silent for a pause then burst out cackling."

"I'm going too. I love you too, sis," she says stressing the word for fun, side hugs me, and bounces away into the crowd.

When I have the buffet full, I pull clean plates out of the dishwasher, set them out, then load the dirty ones, and start them washing. We might need them. No paper plates for my family, even if it is acceptable these days. Jacob wanders into the kitchen with some of the wait staff to get some water. He's wiping his forehead of sweat and asks, "Vanessa, are you having any fun or just helping the staff?"

"I'm finished here, but Jacob, I'd like to go meet my boyfriend. He's waiting for me under the bridge. I wanted you to meet him, but I'm afraid Nina will cause a scene."

He huffs and takes an even deeper breath and grimaces. Blinking he says, "I'm sorry for upsetting you this week. Will you please call me dad again? I already know Nina is a drama queen, but I do love her, and she loves me. Why would she cause a scene?"

I look at my hands, rub them together, and decide to come clean. "Because, Dad, my boyfriend, is the Cave Bear quarterback… Jimmy Danforth." I squint one eye waiting for the ball to drop.

There's a pregnant pause as my dad starts to chuckle. It turns to an all-out hysterical wheeze fest. As his laughter fades, he wipes his tearing eyes. "Well, kid, when you are right, you're right. Personally, you can't blame the kid for being born to the parents he has. Nina would die, and so would you from her glare. I'll make excuses for you if she even recognizes you're gone. Go see your boy, but don't be out all night, and take a jacket it's getting cold. In fact, take one of those baskets under the bar and fill it with food and drink, and take a blanket. Tell me tomorrow if you like the fireworks, even if it's just in a text. I really do love you, young lady," he says kissing me on the forehead before leaving the room.

Not waiting for my good fortune to fade, quick as a shot, I get the basket filled, grab a picnic blanket from the pantry, put on my jacket, and sneak out the side door.

WHEN I STROLL up to the bridge, there's my boy. I wait for a second and take in the view. The bridge is a metal train bridge, not big just long enough to cross the river, about the length of a football field maybe a bit larger. The night sky is dark and contrasts beautifully with the bright twinkling stars. Jimmy was right, I can hear the party music and a little of the noise from the crowd.

I'm am a fortunate girl. As if he hears my thoughts, he raises his head and watches me half run to him with my basket. I set it on a blanket he has put there with a couple of pillows. He reaches out his arm for me to snuggle up. I don't have to be asked twice.

"Hmmm, this is nice. How did you get here? Did Joe bring you, Jimmy?" I question with my face pressed against his chest, the fresh smell of citrus and clean draws me in deeper.

He rocks me gently and says, "Yes, I told him I'd text if I need a ride, but not to count on it. I don't mind sleeping out here under the bridge just to be close to you."

"I won't let you do that, even if it's not that cold. It is too cold to sleep out here, and you don't have a big enough blanket. If nothing else, I'll sneak you into the pool house. I told my dad about you, and he's okay with us. He told me to pack this food. Do you want something to drink? I brought us some soda?"

"Wow, Ness. You told your dad? Thank you, it makes me feel good. Don't get me wrong I didn't think you were ashamed of me. I know for sure you aren't now if that makes any sense. And yep, I do, hand me a coke, please."

I reach into the basket and hand him a coke and get me out a lemonade at the same time. The music changes, and we hear Theory's "Bad Girlfriend" booming across the way. I chuckle and say, "I can just see Cilla dancing on a table right about now."

Jimmy hoots some too and says, "Your sisters are fun when they want to be. I hope you're really okay that they're moving so far away."

"It's the best thing that could happen for me. Nina is terrible and hates me. They'll be back in a few weeks to get more stuff and check things out. I bet they're back and forth several times this year. I can always travel too. Do you want to go to France with me after we're eighteen, so Nina has no say?"

"I'd love to be anywhere you are, anytime, as long as school and sports allow," he almost whispers. He's getting closer and is about to kiss me. I can tell he's going slow, so I can say no if I want to. Instead, I lean into him and press my lips to his first. His hand snakes around my waist. The lapping of the water and his breathing are all I can hear now. I'm falling hard for this boy. He deepens the kiss and leans me back on the blanket, covering me with his body. Why did I think it was cold out here?

Suddenly, a loud boom goes off, and we jerk away from each other as the first fireworks explode. I watch as streaks of bright lights mount the star-strewn night and as the explosions of the fireworks burst and sizzle above us. Jimmy tightens his arm around me, and we lay down to watch the beautiful light show.

His arm is hot where he's touching me, and his hand is on my stomach. No matter how beautiful the fireworks are, I can't think of anything but him. I rotate onto his chest and kiss his sexy mouth again. He rolls me back, putting his weight on me. Oh crap, that feels so good. My legs automatically separate to make room for him, his tongue dancing with mine. Our heartbeats speed up with our breathing, and my hips grind into his. Holy crud, that feels amazing. Way better than when I touch myself. He grinds into me, and we get a rhythm going, slow and tender. The fireworks crackle, boom, and pop in the background and an unusually large boom jerks us back to reality.

He stares into my eyes. His brows knit with a serious look. Then he rolls away and draws me close under his arm, and we watch the rest of the show without a word between us. We silently enjoy being close together in the night with a beautiful display in the sky. When the show is over, he says, "Ness, I love you." He pauses then continues, "I don't expect you to say it to me if you don't love me yet. I don't want to pressure you at all. In fact, I'd like to talk seriously now if that's okay with you?"

"Jimmy John Danforth, I do love you. You aren't forcing me to tell you that, and you're right, we need to discuss this relationship. I'm sorry I got you all ready for sex, and I know you think I'm not ready, but I am, and I want you to be my first." I look away when I say the last just in case he doesn't really want me that way, but I look back to see if there's a chance he does. The pain on his face is evident. My heart falls, and I try to scoot away from him, but he holds me tight and won't let me get away.

He says quietly, "No, Nessa, you aren't understanding. I want you, and if you were eighteen now, I would be fucking you until you scream my name. The fact is I'm eighteen, and you're underage by law. If your stepmom found out... and believe me they have ways, I could go to prison for statutory rape. At the very least, I could get a sex offender charge for life. Your parents have a lot of pull in this community, and I have no doubt that Nina would see me arrested if she knew. It doesn't change how much I want you, or that I'll have blue balls until you are of age. If you even still want me, then?"

"I understand, and you're right. You don't have to ask if I'll still want you, I will. We do have to wait. I want you that way, right now. And while you may have blue balls, I'm going to have wet dreams!" *What! I can't believe I said that.* I can't hold back my snort of glee. Jimmy's obviously more relaxed and spits coke as he laughs at me. We kiss gently one more time before relaxing back on the blanket.

After some time, we get out some of the food, eat, and enjoy each other's company until the sun begins to rise. We stayed up all night, the time passed before I knew it. We watch the sunrise in each other's arms. Then his phone beeps and he has a text from Joe who says he'll be here in fifteen minutes to pick him up. Jimmy responds with a 'thumbs up' emoji. Now, the trick will be for me to get back inside my house without Nina killing me.

On second thought, I couldn't care two shits about what Nina thinks. What a great Valentine's Day. I'll never forget it, it was fireworks.

17

THE FAMILY

Jimmy and I have everything packed and are standing hand in hand near the railroad tracks, waiting for Joe to show up. When he gets here, he lets us know that a bunch of the kids are going to the Sheriff's Posse Arena tonight for a bonfire and we're invited. The Sheriff's Posse Arena is a place in the country where we have rodeos and sometimes pow wows. They say Wild Bill did his show there in the early 1900s. Today, teens go there and drive down a dirt road to an open patch of ground behind the arena and have bonfires and parties. If the authorities knew they would raid us, so we keep all of them a secret and break it up after a few hours.

I make a date to pick Jimmy up. We decide we'll drive out there later this evening to meet the other kids. As it is, I need to get myself home and clean like the dickens, so Nina lets me out of the house tonight.

I sneak up to the back of the house, which is the farthest away from Dad and Nina's room. This party mess is impressive, and I'm surprised Nina let the wait staff leave before it was immaculate. I set the basket on a table and walk into the house and change into work clothes.

My shadow hadn't yet had the chance to catch up to me entering the kitchen, and Kate is waiting with her hand out holding a large steaming cup of coffee with my favorite creamer already stirred in. As I take the cup and thank her, she turns back to the stove to scoop me out a dish of breakfast casserole. The young cook slides it in front of me, along with a plate of fresh toast. She even remembers my favorite blackberry jam. I shouldn't be hungry, but I eat and love it.

When I finish my surprise breakfast, coffee included, I head out to the patio to start to clean up. It just might get me out of the house tonight without a fight. My eighteenth birthday isn't that far away, in fact just over a month, but I don't want a battle to point that out. It would be nice if they knew though.

I say, "Kate, I'm going to clean the patio. I want to go out without a fight from Nina tonight. I wonder why she didn't have the staff clean up last night?"

"She said she noticed that you hadn't come out of your room all night to be with your sisters, so you could do it to make it up to them," she answers with a sour twist of her lips. "Your life will be easier when they move, Nessa. I wish it weren't so hard on you now."

My phone rings so I nod at her and answer it, "Granny, how are you... yes... I'll see you this evening, then."

"Awesome, my Granny just gave me the perfect reason to be out of the house tonight. She asked if I'd come over and help her fix her hair for a night out with friends."

"I think things are going in your favor, girl. I'd still get on that patio before your stepmother wakes up though, just to cement the deal," Kate says.

I'M PUTTING the outdoor brooms away in the shed by the boathouse when I hear yelling. I run up to the house, then wish I hadn't. I walk in on Nina yelling at the pool boy for the cover being rusted closed. She wants him to force it open to get it moving and start getting it ready for summer. I stop dead in my tracks just as Dad walks out. This is my chance, so I say, "Hey, Dad, Granny called and wants me to come over tonight. I might be late getting home and might just spend the night with her and Papa."

Nina starts, "Not on your..."

When Dad cuts her off saying, "What a wonderful idea. Tell them I said hi and give them a big hug from us. What time are you leaving, before or after dinner?"

"Right now, actually, as soon as I clean up a bit," I answer giving him a quick hug and a covert wink scooting by him and into the house.

Nina is huffing and stammering, but I shut the door on the noise and get the fastest shower of my life. Then I dress and put on a five-minute face of makeup before I pack a little bag. The kitchen is full of people, including Nina, and they all see me when I start into the room, so I can't back out. This is a challenge I can get through, so I skip up to Dad and hug him and say, "I'll be home tomorrow before lunch."

If looks could kill, I'd be one dead girl. It isn't lost on Dad, and he gives me a break by responding, "Don't worry, sweetheart. You haven't spent time with your grandparents in a while, so take whatever time you need. We're going to be packing anyway. I'll see you when you get home."

Cilla and Cess, both wave and shout, "Bye!" and "Have fun!" as I walk out. Pulling my car out of the drive, I see that the pool boy is getting in his own vehicle to leave also. I stop and say, "Did you get it all figured out?"

He says, "Yes, and I never want to come back here and deal with your mom again. She almost hit me."

I reply, "Step-monster, not mom, and no one knows how you feel more than I do. She won't be here that much after tomorrow. They're moving to France, and it'll be just me. They'll be back periodically though so you might see her. I would appreciate it if you did come back though."

"That is great news. I was ready to tell my boss we can do without this job. If you don't mind, I'll call before I come next time just to verify!"

"I understand, here, let me give you my cell just in case." I tap my number into his phone, he grins, and thanks me before getting back in his truck and leaving. I text Jimmy before I head out of the drive.

ME: I'm on the way to pick you up. If you don't mind meeting Granny and Papa with me, that is. But... if you would rather wait, that works too.

Him: Hurry, I'm bored.

HE'S WAITING for me in Joe's yard. He runs up to the car, and we take off like we had just committed a bank robbery. Okay, so maybe not that fast. My car is old, and Nina doesn't let my dad put much money into it. Just enough to keep it road worthy...

"I'm going to my grandparents if you don't mind. My Granny needs help fixing her hair tonight, and I want them to meet you if you don't mind?" Why do I keep saying, "If you don't mind..."? This boy has made a mumbling mess of my brain.

"Ooo, meeting the grandparents! I'm okay with that. Then do you want to get something to eat before we go to the Sheriff's Arena?"

His comment takes me to the task at hand, drive and talk without sounding like an overgrown ninth grader with her first crush. "Yes, if you don't mind a drive through. I sort of told Dad and Nina that I'll be with Granny and Papa tonight. I don't want to chance them seeing us."

"Hmmm, so we're going covert? I like it, wild woman." He's chuckling at me.

Cueva Hallow isn't large, and my grandparents don't live that far away. Within a few minutes, we're pulling into their drive. The house is in one of the better parts of town, but way up on one of the hills away from most neighbors. It's lined with trees... evergreens, fruit trees, pecan trees. Even if the fruit trees are bare right now from the winter, this plot of heaven is still beautiful.

I pat Jimmy on the leg as we get out and say, "They're going to love you. You'll know as soon as Granny tries to feed you."

We hold hands on the way to the door. I never have knocked, but I ring the bell anyway. We walk in, and both my grandparents are sitting in the front room reading. They look up and smile when they see me. I hug them both and introduce Jimmy. He shakes their hands then we sit down on their flowered patterned couch to visit.

18

THE BONFIRE

ONE TOPIC WHICH INEVITABLY COMES UP WHEN I VISIT MY grandparents is how things are at home. They already know that Nina isn't easy on me.

I say, "I almost asked if I could come to live with you, then they decided they would move the twins to a girls academy in France. I should probably feel bad that they're leaving, but I don't."

Granny calmly looks me over and with her genuine little smile says, "You always have a place here with us if you need it. Never be afraid to ask if you need to. Now, will you please come and help me with my hair? We need to leave at five to be at Papa's company party. You know he doesn't like being late," she snickers. Only her whole upper body is moving up and down, her mouth screwed up beautifully. When Granny laughs, you know she means it. She gets up and adds, "I better go change and get ready. Jimmy, you can stay with Papa or go search the fridge and find something to eat."

That's enough for me. I'm sure she likes him and give him a covert nod as I scoot out of my chair to follow her to her extra-large bathroom. She sits in front of her vanity. We've done this before, so I know where all of her tools are and get them out. I plug them in turning them on at the same time.

She gazes at me in the mirror, and I stare back as she says, "Vanessa, your boy loves you already, can you tell?"

I blink and take a quick breath and answer, "I sure hope that's the case, Gran, because I'm falling fast and hard for him."

"Well, if nothing else, he is cute! You have great taste. He reminds me of Papa when we were young. Not that blond hair but those pale blue eyes and his muscular form. Papa's hair was always dark."

I don't even try to hide my side grin and say, "He is cute, isn't he? You have good taste too, Gran. I told Dad that I was staying with you so I could stay out all night and not go home until they're leaving for the airport. Not because I don't love them, but you know how hard it can get with Nina and I don't want her to make me do all the packing for them. She'll blame me if something she wants isn't there."

"I understand. I'm not sure about you staying out all night with a boy, though."

"Well, just so you know, it'll be for talking and going places not sex, Gran. We talked about that and are planning to wait. You and I both know that Nina would have no problem having him arrested to ruin my life."

"Okay, that's good to hear. Just come and stay here if you don't have enough to do and come back for breakfast with us. I'll have Papa take us out. How does eight o'clock sound? You can meet us at the Jamison Hotel, bring Jimmy."

"Oh, I love that place and never get to go there. Their breakfast buffet is my favorite. We'll be there if Jimmy says yes. If he can't, I'll be there." I continue fixing her hair and put it up in an updo. I add a jeweled comb and stand back to look as she says, "Whatever your career choice is, you could always do hair on the side, Nessie. My hair has never looked better!"

"I'm not one hundred percent sure, but I want to do something in government. Maybe an ambassador. Wouldn't that be a kick? Nina would hate me for sure if I were the French ambassador for the United States. It still sounds so fun and something I would love."

"There isn't anything you can't do. You are so like your mama in that. Tell me what dress to wear now. I need to look good. Papa's going to be playing the guitar, and I'm going to sing with the band. Isn't that a hoot?"

"You're kidding me, Granny! That's so cool! What's the name of the band?"

She beams and says, "We call ourselves Granny and the Dirt Angel Band. We aren't famous, but we have fun!"

My pearly whites shine back at her when I say, "Wonders never cease, you'll kill it. I'm so proud of you."

She scoots her chair under the vanity and says cutely, "Oh, go on."

We walk into her closet area just off the bathroom and pick a coral blouse, and cream-colored pants then get her pearls for the piece de resistance. When we walk into the living room where Papa and Jimmy are, Papa whistles at her.

I hold back a snicker as Jimmy tells her she looks lovely. Papa gets up and puts on his suit coat then his long coat and gloves. He reaches into the closet and retrieves Granny's long coat then helps her into it.

She pulls a designer scarf out of the pocket and puts it on saying, "I can't take a chance the weather will mess my hair before anyone has a chance to glimpse how beautiful it is." She puts on her own gloves as Jimmy and I put on our jackets as we get ready to leave too. I have to move my car first, or they won't be able to get out of the driveway. After hugs Jimmy and I are off and on our way to the bonfire to see our own friends.

WHEN WE PULL behind the Sheriff's Posse Arena, I spy a red ribbon tied on one of the bushes and know I'm headed in the right direction. Further up the road I see another and keep on the track. I spot other vehicles up ahead and park next to them. Wow, there are a lot of people here. I get my defensive face on as we get out. I've found it's easier to appear stuck up, so I don't get asked out by every guy I meet. They might still try to flirt but not as many as when I am even the least bit friendly to them, even though it's widely known I'm with Jimmy.

Jimmy walks up to some of his friends on the football team. I go with him holding onto his arm. The ground isn't flat here, and it gives me an excuse to touch him.

He says, "Hey, guys."

They say in unison, "Hey."

Zane pipes up, "I brought some tequila and salt and lime for shots. What did you bring Jimmy? And hi, Vanessa, how ya doing?"

I nod my head to Zane when Jimmy answers him and says, "We weren't planning on drinking, just having some fun and hanging out. We did bring a case of Coke and another of Sprite to share though. They're in the cooler in the trunk."

Zane has already been sampling the wares if I don't miss my guess, he slurs as he replies, "What, and ruin the party. You have to drink a shot with me, at least one, or I'll label you whipped already."

Jimmy's face screws up in a wave of anger and he's about to respond to the insult when Caro drives up and sprays us all with a fine mist of dirt and gravel. She gets out of her truck, and the whole cheer squad piles out after her. They run, skip, and bounce over to us.

Caro exclaims, "I'm so sorry guys. I didn't mean to throw so much dirt up. I'll make it up to you if you pitch in, because I brought a keg!"

"We're okay but we weren't planning to drink," I say.

"Ahh, come on Ness, you only live once. Loosen up will ya?" she whines.

Jimmy nods to me with a grin and says, "It's up to you, beautiful."

There are cheers all around, as I take a twenty out of my pocket and give it to her for Jimmy and me and say, "Here you twisted woman this is mine and Jimmy's buy-in for the beer. Who bought it for you, and what kind did you get?"

She laughs and says, "My brother got it for me if I babysit for free for the summer. He got Michelob Light, so we can save a few calories at least. I heard the boys were bringing tequila for shots."

It's starting to get dark, and the boys and Dice are lighting the bonfire. They have a pile of old pallets taller than them soaked with lighter fluid. It takes on the first match and starts the blaze moving all over the wood. We have the people with trucks back into the circle so we can sit on the tailgates.

Joe taps the keg Caro brought, and it isn't the only one. Some of the other trucks have barrels in the back and crowds of kids are already drinking from blue Dixie cups that the cheerleaders brought. Joe picks Caro upon his shoulders, and she shouts, "Everyone this is for fun, but we have to keep it clean or the authorities will start watching for this type of party and won't turn a blind eye. So, make sure your trash goes into a truck bed or preferably into the trash bags in mine... this has been a public service announcement."

She laughs, and Joe spins with her grinning as she hangs on to him tighter. He lets her off by getting close to her tailgate so she can step off.

The night moves on, and several others show up and park behind the cars and trucks already here. There are so many. We're having a great time. My boyfriend is sitting on the back of Caro's truck by me and kisses me. I'm a little buzzed from the alcohol but not bad. Not like most of this crowd who are sloshed. Several of the kids are stumbling around and bumping into people, so Jimmy jumps down and sits them down against some rocks that are part of the area. When they're comfortable, he comes back and puts a hand on my leg and says, "You ready beautiful? I think we should leave."

He no sooner gets the words out when we hear the whine of sirens and see lights approaching. "Fuck a duck!" Jimmy hollers.

I watch as several of the kids jump in their vehicles and speed off. My Mustang is blocked in, and I can't get out, but we're in the car in a flash. "Come on, guys, move it!" I yell.

We're too late. The sheriffs block the road, going both ways and are arresting people. An officer knocks on my window, motioning to roll it down. I do and give him our IDs, and he has us get out and take a sobriety test. I trip on a tree root, and that's enough for the officer to arrest me. Jimmy fails on purpose, and we're hauled off in the back of a sheriff's vehicle.

My heart is in my throat. I'll be in so much trouble. I think I should call Granny and Papa, but I can't do that to them and the Dirt Angels so when it's time, I call my dad. This is going to be bad.

"Dad," I choke out.

"Vanessa is everything alright. Are you hurt? Is it your grand-parents?"

I start to cry, "No, Dad, the sheriff arrested Jimmy and me for going to a bonfire and drinking underaged and attempting to evade arrest." I said it all wrong and hoped he understood me.

"I'll be right there," he says using his dad voice. I don't know whether to be happy or scared. I'm relieved, though.

19

JAIL BIRDS

DAD PAID MY BAIL, AND AFTER I BEGGED, HE PAID JIMMY'S. HE'S blaming Jimmy for being a bad influence, and I'm grounded for the rest of my life. He took me back to my car and says, "Go drop off your friend, then go straight home no detours little miss, and I mean it."

I pull up to Joe's house, and Jimmy gets out and says, "I'm sorry, Ness. Tell them it was all me if you have to."

"I'm not doing that. If I get to keep my phone, I'll text you later. Jimmy, thank you for staying with me."

"What, were you afraid I'd take off with Joe and leave you by yourself? Never, I love you too much to do that." Joe walks out and waves, his shoulders drooping. Jimmy pecks me on the cheek and walks off with his head hanging. I hope he isn't thinking he let me down.

The road home is clear. There isn't anyone out this early. I pull into my spot, cover my car, and wait outside the door. Tears pour down my face. I've messed up so much I have to be kind and take my lumps.

I open the door, and Dad is sitting at the bar waiting for me with a glass of water that he hands to me with a couple of aspirin. I take them as he says, "I'm disappointed, to say the least. I don't know what to do, Vanessa, if your... Nina finds out about this... well needless to say we will be in hell. I know she's hard on you, but what you did is such a letdown. Tell me what happened to get you into that situation. I thought you were going to your grandparents."

I tell him the entire story, even the part about Granny knowing and that I'm supposed to meet her and Papa for breakfast. Then I say, "Dad, I'm so sorry. I didn't even go to drink and wasn't going to, I just did. I don't even know why. Maybe to be part of the crowd."

"It might surprise you, but I do understand. Did you know that your mom and I got arrested once in the same kind of circumstances? We were with friends, and I was very drunk. My dad made me stay in jail all night. I never really forgave him for that, while I was there I was beaten up pretty bad..." He trailed off, and I got the idea there was more he wasn't saying.

"I'm so sorry, Dad." I give him a real hug from the heart then add, "I deserve whatever punishment you dole out. I'll take it and do my best to do better from now on. I know it was stupid."

"Vanessa, I do have a way for you to pay me back. First, this is a secret between us. I don't want Nina to find out. Second, I want you and your boyfriend to work for my company after school to pay off your debts. You'll be in a document control area and used as gofers and delivery people. It won't be prestigious. Third, if you could please, I need you to come to France during the holidays so we can be a family. I don't want this separation to make the rift bigger. Nina can be hard to handle, yes, but when you really get to know her, she has depths no one sees unless they try. I know she really loves me and she's a great asset in the company because she is a shrewd businesswoman..."

I put my hand on my dad's arm and say, "You got it, Dad. You don't have to defend her. I know she loves you. She just doesn't like me. I'll do my best."

He hugs me, and I listen to his heartbeat under his soft tee. It's been so long since I felt like he loved me. I can't help being a baby as tears slide silently down my face. I back away before he notices and says. "I love you, Dad, but I really need some sleep. I'm picking up Jimmy and meeting Gran in a few hours."

"Goodnight then daughter, I enjoyed getting to talk to you like this again." He slides off the bar stool and walks into his own room. I hear Nina ask if everything is alright. Dad tells her he has a stomach ache and was getting some Pepto.

I smile and open my door silently then text Jimmy that it's okay I'll explain what happened when I pick him up at 7:30 for breakfast.

He sends back a heart.

BREAKFAST WAS FANTASTIC, and I was starving. I told Granny the whole story. I don't think Papa heard a word. He's a social butterfly and spent a good deal of time visiting with other people all around the restaurant after he ate. If he had heard, he would have lectured me for hours. Gran isn't that way. She laughed and shared a story about what she and Papa had done in a similar situation. No matter how old I get, my grandparents continue to surprise me.

After breakfast, I took Jimmy home and go home to say goodbye to my family. It will be a change.

There are a ton of suitcases by the door when I get there.

Nina says, "Well, I wasn't sure if we were important enough to you to merit a goodbye, Vanessa."

I take the jibe. I told Dad I would try to get along with her better, and I will. I answer, "There's no way I'd let you all go without a hug."

The twins sniff as I give them hugs. Cess says, "You will come and see us, right? I'll miss you."

There is a loud honk just as Cilla tells me much the same. Nina gives me a fast embrace and says, "Let the driver in girls, so he can pack our cases, and go wait in the car." Then she faces me and adds, "I had new cameras installed throughout the house, so if you think you will be getting away with big parties or worse think again."

I take a deep breath and say, "I'll do my best to behave and take care of your house, Nina. Have a safe trip."

Dad rolls his eyes at her and grabs me up in a big hug. He says, "Take care my daughter. I'm only a phone call away. If you need me, I can be home in a day. I love you, little girl."

I sniff and say, "I love you too, Daddy."

Then they're gone. The sunlight fades, and the silence is deafening.

20

LIFE GOES ON

GETTING UP TODAY IS A MIXED BAG FOR ME. IT'S A RELIEF NOT having to worry about Nina getting mad at me or treating me like a leper. But the quiet is almost oppressive. I'm not going to let a lack of sound bring me down today. Besides, if I need noise, I can turn on the stereo to my favorite station and turn it up. There, noise problem solved!

When I get to school, it's busy, but the teachers take it easy on us by not giving out much homework. Jimmy's just finishing up football practice, and I'm sitting in the bleachers, my cheer practice over before his by a long shot. I watch him and can't get over the fact he's my boyfriend. Every time he bends over, I'm drawn to his butt and the bump of his boy stuff. I gulp and think of liver. I hate liver. I hate liver. When they finish, he points to the locker room then at me before racing off to shower and change.

A cold, dry desert wind is picking up and blowing dust around, so I decide to wait for him in my car. I've learned to be cautious and lock the door after I get in. When I settle down, I take out my phone to read a book on my Kindle app. I'm just getting into a contemporary romance called *Memphis* by Kelly Walker when I hear a tap on my passenger window.

Oh, those baby blues are killer. I unlock the door for the most attractive boy on the planet, he gets in and says, "Hey beautiful since we don't have to work today how about we go to the Pasta Joint for some dinner? I got paid this weekend from the newspaper and want a date with my baby. I might not get covered in primavera this time."

"I still have the gift card to use that the manager gave us. Just make sure I remember to plop it down and tell them before we order, so they know. And I hope you don't get covered in pasta again too!" I giggle remembering the last trip there.

It's getting windy when I get out of the car, my hair flies around my head. Jimmy is behind me in seconds covering me with his body to break the wind. I remember the last time we were here, and Mrs. Hashtag's dress blew up and giggle. My boy opens the door for me and smiles knowingly.

The waitress from before recognizes us right off and seats us asking, "Can I take your drink orders first?"

"I want lemon water, and we have our gift card from the last trip to use tonight if that's all right."

She says, "That's fine, I'm glad you remembered it." She looks over at Jimmy and asks, "And for you, young man, what can I get you?"

"I'll take a Coke and water too, please."

"And you want bread, right?" she adds.

We nod, and she's off. Minutes later, she returns with our drink order along with the bread and a plate of spices. We know what we want and order before she leaves. The olive oil is sitting on my right, so I pour it over the spices and we start breaking off pieces of the bread. Yum, that is so good.

As we sit, we talk about the new jobs that Dad gave us. We'll start next weekend. Our waitress reappears with our food and pretends to stumble, lifting a plate toward Jimmy. He instinctively raises a hand to grab it. She's snickering and says, "Sorry, I just had to."

I say, "Now that's funny, but I'm glad you were joking."

We eat, and I ask, "Jimmy, my parents are gone, and I want you to come to stay with me. There is a slight problem, though. Nina had cameras installed around the house. I can't be sure where they all are, and I know she will be checking them."

"No problem Nessa, Joe is a wiz at hacking, and I bet he won't mind resetting the system to show only in the day hours and loop stills at night when I'm there or on weekends. I'll text him and see what he's up to. His phone beeps in seconds, and Joe says he'll meet us there in fifteen minutes. Perfect timing since we're finished with our meal. We get chocolate cake to go and thank them before heading to my house.

When we're in the car we make a plan, I say, "Now when we get there we need to sit at the bar in the kitchen and look like we are doing homework. Then Joe can come over to do *homework* with us. I need it to look like you both leave on the cameras before the loop kicks in though. How is that?"

"I think it sounds fine, beautiful. Joe will know what we need to do."

That's exactly how it plays out. Thanks to Joe, we can access the cameras on both of our phones, controlling and viewing whenever we want. The boys walk out the door, and our genius hacker friend resets the cameras to show a dummy blank view before Jimmy and I walk back inside.

Jimmy pats Joe on the back and says, "I owe you one. I can't thank you enough. Have a great night, and I'll see you tomorrow."

Joe responds, "Sure, anything for you. Yeah, I'll see you tomorrow."

Jimmy and I go back in and verify that the cameras don't show us. Then we sit and eat our cake and drink milk. "Jimmy, you can have the guest bedroom by my room. I can keep the deal we made to wait until my eighteenth birthday for your protection, but after that, I might not want to anymore. I think about you a lot."

"Nessa, thank you for protecting me. I think about you too, and even being in another room is still a challenge. I'm ready for bed now though if you are."

"I am." I kiss him goodnight and go to my room. After I'm lying there, all I can think about is him. *I wonder if this will ever get easier?*

21

THE FIRE

THREE WEEKS LATER...

WE'RE TRYING TO STAY AWAY FROM MY HOUSE JUST TO BE ON the safe side. It's getting closer to my birthday, and our hormones are driving us crazy! Somehow, we're sticking with the deal. At my request, Jimmy takes me on a drive in the country after school. We decide to stop and park in Courtin' Canyon, a place famous for teen rendezvous.

"Jimmy, I let you drive my car so we could go fast since I can't do it. Even without my sling that Dr. Vargas said to quit using last week, my arm is still tender. Now, would you go fast? We're in the country, no one will stop us."

"Okay, but you said it, babe! Here we go!" He pushes the pedal to the metal, and we zoom ahead, leaving a dust cloud in our wake. When we get to a dip in the road, Jimmy speeds over it. The car takes air... well, at least it feels like it does. We both pop up as far as the seat belts allow. Jimmy's head touches the roof of the Mustang.

"My stomach's in my throat. That's so fun! Do it again!" I say.

He's laughing and whoopin' as he continues on. "Babe, I need to park. The dust is filling my eyes!" Then he pulls down a dirt road into Courtin' Canyon and parks in a stand of trees.

I slump in my seat and say, "I think I'm addicted. That's fun. Maybe, I should train to be a race car driver. What do you think?"

"I think you should give me a kiss." His sly grin and bright eyes are all it takes to set my already sensitive tummy tingling.

I reach over and put my hands on his face and say, "With pleasure." It stretches into minutes and shirts are raising up when I croak, "No wonder people complain about the gear shift. It's pressing into my side, babe."

"Here, Nessa, let's get into the back seat."

"Okay, he helps me out of the car and asks, "Can you smell smoke?"

I shake my head side to side while looking around, sniffing and wrinkling my nose up. "No, I don't smell anything."

He gets in the back seat and pulls me onto his lap. I willingly go, and my hands rest on his chest, all of my weight now on him. "Am I squashing you? Can you breathe?"

"You don't weigh enough to squash me. I can breathe fine. I'm not a weakling, Nessa." He puts both his hands up and slides them into my hair. As he reaches the back of my head, he pulls my face close. His kisses are amazing in general, but these are shocking in their sensuality. I feel bursts of pleasure deep inside. My mind is racing, and my hormones raging. I groan in pleasure and open my mouth to take him in. He takes that as an invitation and plunges his tongue in. This kiss is strong and deep.

Unwillingly, I pull away and take off my shirt and say, "Take it off."

He doesn't wait a second and reaches with one hand and pulls off his tee. I have to catch my breath and swallow hard as I stare at his hard-athletic body. I can't resist, and I run my hands over his muscled chest. He jumps when I hit him in just the right spot.

"Oh sorry, did that, tickle?"

"No, it felt good."

With forethought, this time, I silkily repeat the movement. This time, a deep breathy moan escapes his mouth.

I lean into him and start kissing him again. My body moving rhythmically on him feeling his hardness pushing against me. When I take off my bra and glance at him, his eyes are enormous. I enjoy the effect I'm having on him, his Adam's apple moves as he tries to swallow then he leans into me, licks one nipple, and sucks it into his mouth. With his other hand he begins to firmly roll my other nipple between his fingers.

"Holy crap, that feels good!" I put both hands in his hair and stop dead still. I stop when I hear a crackling sound. I open my eyes to make sure no one is coming to the car. "Wait, I do smell smoke, now. Oh, no, look!"

Jimmy is already glancing out the window to see what the problem is and says, "It's a fire, and it's close."

The pause is slight, and when it's over, he is moving quickly. "Oh, shit. Nessa get dressed fast." He takes a pocket knife out and cuts his tee shirt into pieces. Then grabbing his water bottle from the front seat, he dumps it on the pieces. I get my bra back on, and I'm reaching for my shirt when we hear a whirring crackling sound. I immediately know it is trees popping from the nearby fire.

Suddenly we hear a loud screeching of metal tearing. When it's done, the top of my car is gone, and I watch as a red devil with wings that had to span fifteen feet, reaches for me. For some reason, I let him. His muscles have muscles, and he feels like a rock. I turn my head and see that a huge blue guy with a blond mohawk is here too, and he's picking up Jimmy.

The last thing I remember is an odd singing and getting sleepy. I slump into the red monster who has me. Oddly, I feel like I passed into a hazy dream... then I black out.

WHAT FEELS LIKE SECONDS LATER, I'm waking up at the Ranger's Station. What the fuck? How in the ever-loving hell did we get here? It must have been those guys who saved us.

An officer is helping Jimmy. I examine the beautiful lady near him. She's stunning. She has long dark hair, and her eyes glimmer gold in the night. I know I can trust this woman, then I hear her say...

"Hi there, I'm Officer Macbard. How do you feel?"

Jimmy reaches for my hand for comfort. He must be as stumped as I am, because his mouth is hanging open.

I take charge and begin, "I'm feeling fine. I know this sounds weird, but the devil just saved my boyfriend and me from a fire in Courtin' Canyon up on Deer Ridge. He was with a huge blue monster. They tore the roof right off my car to save us. I don't remember anything after that until I woke up here. It just happened. I guess you already called the fire in, it was traveling fast. We didn't even have time to get out of it. If it wasn't for the devil, I hate to think what would've happened to us." I stop my verbal vomit when I see the ranger roll her eyes. Reflexively, my body stiffens, and I let out an exasperated huff of air. I'm not going to change my story. I'm telling the truth.

Then one of the most gorgeous guys I've ever seen in person saunters up to us and Officer Macbard.

He says, "I have been called many things, ma'am. I might have even been called the devil a time or two. When I pulled you from your car, you were both knocked out. You probably dreamed the devil part. What's your names?"

"Jimmy Danforth and Vanessa Cutter," I answer.

The female ranger says, "Well, Jimmy and Vanessa, it isn't safe right now, so we can't call for someone to pick you up. We'll take you home. I just need to call our boss and check out a vehicle."

Jimmy and I stare at each other. My parents aren't home, but we really don't want anyone knowing he's staying with me. Then Officer Macbard steps away from us with her friend to call her boss so she can check out a vehicle to take us home.

I whisper, "I'll pick you up, have her take you to the diner. I won't tell them my parents aren't home." I nod as small as I can. He nods back. Shit, I'll have to take my dad's car. He won't mind. What he's going to have a fit over is my vehicle being burned to a crisp and how that happened. I hope it doesn't cause them to come home just to ream me, but I bet they do. I'm going to tell everyone about the devil saving us, so maybe someone will tell me who or what that was. I have to know. Where did he come from, and how can I thank him?

THAT NIGHT after I pick Jimmy up from the diner, we talk. Our story is the same. We also both want to know the ones who saved us, at least to say thank you.

I say, "I can't believe there are good monsters."

"Yeah. Me too, I can't believe one that looks like the devil would help us."

"I know, just kills. You know this is going to change everything. I want to figure out who they really are."

"Me too, babe. We need a plan. Let's do some snooping around to figure it out, then maybe we'll find out who they really are."

"Jimmy, I think this might be our grand adventure. I'm down for this as long as it's okay with you... and as far as adventures go, this one might be fun. If I had known what I know now, I would have gotten to our destiny sooner because this is only the beginning!"

ACKNOWLEDGMENTS

Thank you, fans and readers of our books. We appreciate each and every one of you. You are our prize. Please, if you enjoyed the book consider leaving a review. It means more than you can imagine! But if you really hate it... please pass.

Thank you to our family, who is always supportive and helpful. Especially Loren for the band name!

All our friends who are precious to us. Miki and Mine!

Christina and Brenda, you are the best PA's ever!

We love you all. Thank you for your support! — Miki & Garrett Ward

OTHER BOOKS BY MIKI AND GARRETT WARD

The Ceorfan Gargoyles Series

Carved

Etched

Hewn

The Ceorfan Gargoyles Novellas

My Tormented Mage

Shivers Series

We See You

Double Mirror

Elser Books are stand alone

Flesh and Bold

Stand Alone from Miki Ward

My Phantom Queen

Find us

Miki & Mine Facebook Group
https://bit.ly/2CpH3BM

Miki's FB Author page
https://bit.ly/2yMlVSG

Garrett's FB Author page
https://bit.ly/2P3USwv

Instagram
https://bit.ly/2Ro5utp

Bookbub
https://bit.ly/2J3FRFh